FABULOUS HELL

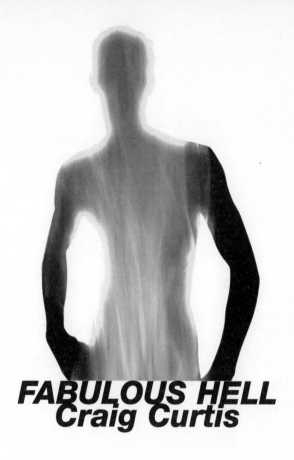

FABULOUS HELL
Craig Curtis

alyson books
los angeles | new york

MANUFACTURED IN THE UNITED STATES OF AMERICA.

THIS TRADE PAPERBACK ORIGINAL IS PUBLISHED BY
ALYSON PUBLICATIONS,
P.O. BOX 4371, LOS ANGELES, CA 90078-4371.
DISTRIBUTION IN THE UNITED KINGDOM BY
TURNAROUND PUBLISHER SERVICES LTD.,
UNIT 3 OLYMPIA TRADING ESTATE, COBURG ROAD, WOOD GREEN,
LONDON N22 6TZ ENGLAND.

FIRST EDITION: APRIL 2000

00 01 02 03 04 **a** 10 9 8 7 6 5 4 3 2 1

ISBN 1-55583-479-5

LIBRARY OF CONGRESS CATALOGING-IN-PUBLICATION DATA
  CURTIS, CRAIG.
    FABULOUS HELL / CRAIG CURTIS — 1ST ED.
    ISBN 1-555583-479-5
    1. GAY MEN—UNITED STATES—FICTION 2. HIV-POSITIVE MEN—
  UNITED STATES—FICTION. I. TITLE.
  PS3553.U695 F33 2000
  813'.6—DC21   99-089537

CREDITS
COVER ILLUSTRATION AND TEXT DESIGN BY B. ZINDA.
AUTHOR PHOTOGRAPH BY STEFANIE SCHNEIDER.

The author gratefully acknowledges the following:

Dennis Colby
Kevin Koffler
The Neals
Ann Easly
Joan Nelson
Cyndi Flock
Dan King
Francisco X. Alarcon
Cherrie Moraga
Terry Wolverton
Nancy Ramos
Scott Brassart
Doran Johnson
Lynn Pfeiffer
Grant Curtis
and
Carolyn See

For Loyce, Chuck, and Merrily

"You might as well live."

—*Dorothy Parker*

AUGUST 1, 1991

The positive test result is given to me by a volunteer in the county clinic in Santa Rosa, California. I am also given a selection of handouts, including information on safe sex, support groups, and proper diet. I am told to limit my alcohol consumption to two ounces per week. I am urged to seek counseling. I am invited to stay and speak with a social worker.

I decline.

Numbly I exit through a rear door. I cannot face the people in the waiting room.

They know.

Upon being informed of the news, Mom insists on traveling from Huntington Beach every other week for two months. I do not want her. She has minimal maternal instincts. I do not trust her.

Mom has hastily prepared a Durable Power of Attorney for Health Care, which I sign, and seen to it that I am written out of my grandparents' will in order to protect the estate from the Powers That Be should I fall ill.

"You know that I will always take care of you," she tells me. I do not.

By her fourth visit our strained relationship falls into disrepair. We do not speak for many months. I'm glad to be rid of her.

I work as a waiter at a gay resort in Guerneville, on the Russian River. I fuck the manager at the time of interview in order to get the job. My subsequent diagnosis has done little to calm my promiscuity.

I wear shorts as part of my uniform. I don't bother to protect myself from hands of vacationing fags who behave like the crazed teenagers in *Palm Springs Weekend*, starring Troy Donahue and Connie Stevens. Tips are great.

Much of my expendable income is spent on cocaine and carousing. I am sexually active, with little sense of responsibility, and free of guilt. I don't care.

I nightly drink eight weeks' worth of my alcohol allotment.

I don't care.

TANG

Food and beverage of my childhood are strange and wonderful things. Twinkies are lighter than air and have creme filling. Wonder Bread is light as well. I like it less for the taste and more for the way it makes little balls of dough when you squish it. These balls are handy for throwing at my little brother. Poor Mark is always getting pelted with things. Steve likes to throw plums at him. They make Mark look like he's been beaten senseless.

Food of the astronauts is immensely popular. I particularly like General Mills Food Sticks. They come in caramel, peanut butter, chocolate, and strawberry. Tasty delish! I find that they trade in the cafeteria like a black-market commodity. Sometimes I can get a tuna sandwich for one. I like tuna better than the peanut butter sandwich Mom packs.

The astronauts stay hydrated with Tang. So do I. Mom makes Russian tea with it. It's the secret ingredient that gives the tea a special *pow*. It's good. It's the only good thing Mom makes. I think she found the recipe in *Woman's Day*.

In the kitchen Mom is a dismal failure. She clips recipes from articles like "Casseroles Every Day of the Week for Pennies a

Serving." This means noodles topped with french-fried onions or crumbled potato chips, baked at 350 degrees. I loathe these taste-less, goopy, one-dish meals. We rejoice when Mom goes back to college: We eat Swanson's frozen dinners. Fried chicken is my favorite.

Mom likes to stay thin, so we do too. She survives mostly on popcorn, and olives soaked in gin. It doesn't seem like much of a diet to me, but she keeps her weight down. My brothers and I are so thin that Grandma bestows care packages of food on the three of us on Christmas and birthdays.

When I graduate from high school, I am 5 feet 11 and weigh 130 pounds.

ORANGE COUNTY

As high season on the Russian River comes to a close, I find myself broke, out of work, and weary from six months of drugging and drinking.

Mom's fourth divorce coincides with my unemployment. She urges me to come home and live with her and a gay couple, Bob and Al. I agree.

I have decided that I am at death's door. So, apparently, has everyone else. Not long after my arrival in Huntington Beach, an extravagant birthday party is given in my honor.

I am presented with a variety of plague-related gifts. Books by Louise Hay. A bathrobe. I smile wanly and accept these tokens of illness. I have learned about dying from films like *Dark Victory*. For the duration of the party, I am poor, brave Bette Davis, valiantly smiling my way to the grave. *Someone! Quick! Pour me some champagne!*

They know.

On further inspection I find that Mom has taken it upon herself to make my business very public.

"They're my friends," she tells me. "Who am *I* supposed to turn to?"

I really don't give a shit, I just know that my information is on the streets. I am not in control.

I attempt to communicate with Mom, Solicitor. "Disclosure of a person's HIV status is illegal."

She stares blankly, unmoved.

"They are my friends. I need them."

The argument goes nowhere.

From this day forward I endure wide eyes and bright smiles. People exclaim, "My *god*, you look *great!*" At church they whisper: "There's poor Marion's boy."

I am invited to a dinner party at which the hostess's son is a no-show; he refuses to dine with a queer, and certainly not with an AIDS victim.

I don't have AIDS!

I don't care.

TELEVISION

Every day I run home from kindergarten to see the last part of *Sheriff John*. If I hurry, I can hear him sing "Put Another Candle on the Birthday Cake." Occasionally Billy Barty is on.

We have a floor-model black-and-white TV on a swivel base. It used to be my grandparents'. Now they have a color set.

When the picture gets distorted, Dad yells at me: "Go get my goddamned screwdrivers." I do. Dad removes the particle board backing from the TV and takes out the tubes. We go to Thrifty, where they have a tube-tester machine. Dad buys the necessary parts, a pint of gin, and a scoop of ice cream on a sugar cone for me.

"Don't tell your mom," he warns as he drinks from the brown paper sack.

"I won't."

On Christmas Day, 1970, we finally get our first 19-inch color set from Sears. It never really works right. From then on it is referred to as The Lemon. I don't like this lemon TV for a couple of reasons. One: It has no remote control. The black-and-white had one; when you hit the channel button, the knob on the set moved. Two: Aside from *Bewitched* my preferred viewing is black-and-white.

I love old movies.

Channel 11 has the best movies, mostly MGM. I watch with square eyes: Judy Garland, Gene Kelly, Katherine Hepburn, and June Allyson. My favorite is Joan Crawford. She has big hair, big shoulders, big eyelashes, big eyebrows, big lipstick, big furs, and big bracelets. She wields big purses, big guns, big axes. She drinks big cocktails and has big fights. She's a goddess.

Channel 9 runs RKO pictures. Yuck. Cheesy Lucille Ball-with-blonde-hair flicks. I like Barbara Stanwyck a lot. She's tough. So is Bette Davis.

I will always watch a Ross Hunter Production and NEVER anything made after 1960. Movies get ugly.

My control over the TV is minimal. I can strong-arm my brothers into watching what I want during the day. At night Dad takes over the set and the couch.

We eat dinner while watching the evening news. I witness the events of the day. I find out about the weather. *LIVE...VIA SATELLITE* I see the war in Vietnam. When Betty Grable dies I recognize a clip from *Moon Over Miami*. Patty Hearst is seen on security cameras clutching a machine gun while robbing a bank. The Hillside Strangler is the stuff that nightmares are made of. So is the Grinch; the Wicked Witch of the West.

My bedtime is 8:30 during the week. I am allowed to stay up until 9 on weekends. If I am quiet, I can sneak into the hallway to watch grown-up shows. I like *Mary Tyler Moore*. I am able to watch the entire world premiere of *Airport* from this vantage point: huddled in shadows, knees to chest, head resting on my knees, lost in the reality of TV.

My reality.

Some nights, in this same position, as my parents wage their bitter war against each other, I pray that morning will come and that Darrin and Samantha Stevens will be my dad and mom.

THE SYSTEM

I need to see a physician. It's been seven months since my last T-cell count and three months since the diarrhea started. I am fatigued and losing weight. The weight loss doesn't scare me (I have a definite alcohol bloat), but the diarrhea is a real nuisance.

I call the county clinic and explain my situation to the chirpy receptionist. She is able to fit me in on the following day.

I arrive early for the appointment. It's a good thing, because there's a stack of documents to be completed, all "strictly confidential," thank-you-very-much.

I survey the waiting area: a couple of cute guys wait anxiously to get tested or to receive results; one straight couple; a Latina with four restless kids; and some extras from *Night of the Living Dead*.

I learn that there is never a hurry in a free clinic. By the time I see the nurse, I have read every pamphlet on the rack, including "STDs & You," "Condom Clues," and "Your Vaginal Warts." Slyly I have a look at the HIV calendar.

In the nurse's cubicle I am handled with rubber gloves. She finds that I have a low-grade fever; mild dehydration.

"Probably from the diarrhea," the nurse explains.

I wish she would explain where she found the frosty-blue eye shadow—and who the HELL permed her hair on TOP of high-lights?!

Next I visit with the doctor. She is straight-haired and thin-lipped. Her manner is severe. She listens as I complain about my runny stool and swabs a spot that may be herpes zoster. "Most peo-ple call them 'shingles,' " she informs me.

I wish I had a curling iron.

Back to the waiting room. Two shady-looking guys stare at me. My, what big pupils they have. I wonder if they are on drugs. For an instant I hunger for what I think they possess.

Now I see the nutritionist. I get The Lecture about diet and answer a few questions about my eating habits. I leave out the part where I survive mostly on candy and scotch.

Finally I am ushered into the social worker's office. Charm pours out of him. He is SO personable, SO concerned, SO delightful.

I fear that I will lapse into a diabetic coma.

He is so friendly, in fact, that I am gleefully lying to him, antic-ipating his next Social Services question.

"Are you sexually active?"

"Oh, no."

"How many partners would you say you've had in the last six months?"

"None."

"Why is that?"

"It wouldn't be proper, my being positive and all." (*Big smile*)

"Do you have any history of substance abuse?"

(*Downcast eyes, hand on chest*) "Never."

For a few moments I am Baby Jane, coquettishly toying with

Edwin, hoping that he will believe I'm the ingenue I am not.

I return in two weeks to learn that I have partied my T-cells from 600 to under 300 in a matter of months.

I don't care.

DAD

Dad is not my father in the biological sense. I came at the age of 2 as part of a package deal.

Mom has me shortly after her 16th birthday. I am the product of a brief marriage to a marine.

At 18 Mom finds that she is again pregnant. She and the father of her second child are married with the understanding that if Dad takes her, he gets both of us. I am adopted. My entire name is changed so that I am no one's Junior. I am named for a prominent TV actor Mom has a crush on.

Until this time I am in the care of my grandparents. I cry bitterly when Mom and Dad take me away. I continue to think of my grandmother as Mom. At 3 Dad forbids her to see me: "He thinks you're his mother, for chrissakes."

Dad is good-looking in a swaggering, tough-guy way. He wears pointy shoes, pegged pants, and greaser-style pompadour long after they are fashionable. He sports a tattoo on his bicep. "Got it in the Navy."

I wonder what the cross and roses mean. I never ask.

Dad is a machinist at a local electronics company. "It's a living," I'm often reminded.

Any work other than manual labor is not "man's work." Accountants and shopkeepers are eyed suspiciously. The salesman who lives across the street with his wife and kids is called "sissy." Mr. Douglas, the school librarian, "ain't right."

I am "princess."

Mom hates this nickname. She hollers "*BUD!*" when Dad starts in. I don't mind. I think of Grace Kelly.

My sexuality is questioned long before I begin to imagine what sex is. Dad starts using "queer" and my name in the same sentence while I am still dragging a yellow plastic bus around the backyard.

The best tactic in dealing with this haranguing is to ignore it completely. Tears bring on the "I'll give you something to cry about" scenes. I become so good at this game that even when held off of the floor by the collar at my throat, I am able to look directly into Dad's fish eyes without feeling a thing.

I feel nothing because I witness these scenes from other parts of the room.

I hover over the bathtub while a little boy is held underwater until his grandmother frees him. I hide in the closet while the boy is fed baby powder until he pukes up orange paste. I peer from behind a potted plant as the boy, beaten with a pepper mill, bleeds into the cracks of the hardwood floor. His mother is concerned for the boy and the floor simultaneously. "I hope this comes up," she angrily tells the man.

I am the keeper of secrets. The secrets are Sacred. "Whatever goes on in this house never leaves the front door," Dad says.

I am happy when we leave the house. Dad loves me. At church Dad puts his arm around my shoulder. In restaurants he cuts my meat into bite-size pieces. Dad gently musses my hair and calls me his "little klutz" when people notice my bruises.

Sometimes at night, when everyone is asleep, I float above a twin bed while a man sodomizes a boy.

Dad loves me.

NOBODY'S BOOZENESS

Alcohol is the recurring theme of my life. My grandparents enjoy happy hour on the patio daily. Mom worships gin and performs the archaic three-martini lunch with religious fervor. I hear through the grapevine that my estranged Dad puts away a case of beer daily. Joan Collins drinks expensive champagne. Nick and Nora Charles indulge in smart cocktails. Pour me a scotch. New roommates drink pink wine from a box by the tumblerful.

Mom meets Al and Bob while I'm residing in Northern California. Al works for the psychiatrist whose office is a few doors down from Mom's.

"They're re-e-eally fun! You're gonna LOVE them," she assures me on the day I move in.

I meet two bleary-eyed booze hounds.

Bob offers up some of the pink nectar, served on the rocks in a large plastic cup inscribed with the Taco Bell insignia. For a second I am in high school, swilling Mad Dog 20/20 in the backseat of a car.

"Your mother's a helluva woah-mun," Bob announces in what I later learn is an Ozark accent. I assume his heritage explains the stemware.

Being a native Californian, I have an elitist attitude toward people from the outside. Although Al is also a native, he hails from a town called Bakersfield, where the dialect can sound strangely like that of any other hillbilly community.

We have rented a large suburban dream home with five bedrooms, three-and-a-half baths, and a swimming pool. The wet bar in the den clinched the deal.

The house is furnished cheaply. Bob and Al insist that the sofa and love seat are "real leather." I know Naugahyde when I see it. I melt down a small corner of the sofa with a lighter to prove my point to Mom.

The "art" collection comes, ready-framed, from a booth at the swap meet. Most of the goose collection is purchased at Pic 'N' Save. Forest green offsets pink. Silk foliage cascades from every available surface. Floral chintz drapes frame each window.

I am living in Fag Hell.

The decor becomes less important when Al (a hobbit with shaved feet) begins to feel comfortable enough to flirt with me. I am aware of his lingering glances. I stiffen when he rubs my shoulder. "You're so tense," he whispers thickly in my ear. I smell the rank fruit of cheap wine on his breath. I think of Dad.

Al regularly offers Xanax to me, which I accept; a fringe benefit of working for a psychiatrist, I presume. Although I am not above fucking someone for street drugs, I'm not about to put out for these oval tablets. Not with him. Not EVEN.

Over martinis I tell Mom that I am uncomfortable being alone with Al.

"It's in your head. He has a boyfriend, you have AIDS. You're just going to have to face it: You're not as attractive as you used to be."

I consider what she tells me as I chomp on an olive. She's right. Who wants broken merchandise? My dating career is over at 27.

"I don't have AIDS."

Mom looks down at her empty glass. Her eye makeup is flawless.

"Waiter, we'll have another round."

The conversation is over.

A few days later Al stumbles into my darkened room and announces that he wants to "grope" me. How thrilling. I rebuff his advance by giving him the I Like You Too Much as a Friend speech. He leers for a moment with bloodshot eyes, turns slowly, and teeters out of the room.

I am not as attractive as I used to be.

HEPATITIS A

The emergency room. I have no insurance and a fever of 105 degrees. My eyes are swollen and I have a throbbing headache. I hear a psychotic buzz.

A steady stream of medical and administrative personnel drift in and out of the cubicle. Some wear protective clothing. A masked, gloved financial administrator in an emerald-green dress apologizes profusely for her garb. "It's not you, really. It's hospital policy."

"I understand." I do understand.

A phlebotomist withdraws a half-gallon of blood from my left arm. It is red. He tells me that I remind him of someone in a Ronald Reagan picture. I do not respond.

I am given a Tylenol suppository and a shot of Demerol. Sleep.

I wake to find Mom, eyebrows knitted together, staring.

"Stop looking at me that way." I feel like I am in a TV movie. I wish she would go away.

Tests show that I am suffering from an allergic reaction to a sulfa drug. Liver in high gear. Hepatitis A. I am admitted and given a private room. HIV can be a wonderful thing.

During the hospitalization I am visited by three resident doctors. I am turned on my sides, poked, and prodded. A lumbar puncture is ordered to ensure that I do not have meningitis. One doctor sighs and shakes his head when I reveal my age. I am discussed in the hallway in hushed tones. I feel like a science experiment.

I have put the word out: no visitors. I ignore the persistent ringing of the phone. Mom does not obey my orders. Nor does Geoff.

Geoff and I met in a nightclub shortly after my relocation to Orange County. During our first date Geoff struggles to tell me that he's HIV-positive. I know what he is going to say before he says it. I watch him squirm and choke out his proclamation. I laugh when he tells me.

We do not become involved romantically. Together we attend movies and art openings. Geoff takes me to an HIV support group. I find that it offers little support. When I tell my sordid story of drugs and promiscuity, the group angrily lashes out.

"You do know that cocaine causes the virus to replicate more quickly."

"You must realize that you are in denial."

Stay tuned for more *Sally Jesse Raphaël*.

In the hospital, I am happy to see Geoff. His new boyfriend stands quietly behind him, watching. I am yellow. I have bed hair. The fluorescent lights and hospital gown do little to improve my pallid complexion; ash has never been a good color for me. I look ill.

After a few minutes of stilted conversation, I am ready to be left alone.

I have received a number of floral arrangements featuring waxy tropical flowers and curly willow. Am I recuperating in an upscale hair salon? I ask the nurse working the graveyard shift to distribute a few of the arrangements to other patients. "I know just where they should go," she tells me. I am satisfied when she later tells me how happy one of her patients was to receive flowers. "He doesn't have anyone."

The sight and smell of fabulous infirmary food makes me nauseous. A foul disposition does little to improve my appetite.

On the fourth day I demand to be released. I want to go home. The doctors advise against it. I am tenacious. I want to go home.

Mom's current boyfriend, Uncle Bill, drives me home. I jokingly refer to all of Mother's boyfriends as "uncle."

"You couldn't stretch out in yer mom's two-seater now, couldja?" This uncle is very jovial.

"Hmph," I reply from the backseat.

At home I camp out on the daybed in the den. Boozy, cheery friends of Mom's pop in to say hello. "You look great" is the usual comment. I invite them in to enjoy tabloid TV with me. Mercifully, no one stays long.

One evening during *Hard Copy*, Mom comes in, a gin-and-tonic clinking in her hand.

"Can I watch?"

Mom hates TV.

I scoot over to make room for her on the bed. She sits very near me; I can't breathe. She touches my arm; I stiffen. She looks at me with drunken concern; I am repulsed. I want to crawl out of myself.

She knows.

She escapes after a few minutes, leaving her cocktail on the floor. She does not return.

I can relax.

BOYS' NIGHT OUT

A new me peers out from the hairdresser's mirror: I'm BLOND! After six weeks in bed, I am in desperate need of a change. I opt for a new 'do.

"Do you like it?"

"It's FABulous," I gush to Elsa as she stands behind me, comb in hand. She wears platform shoes and tight, hip-hugging bell-bottoms. Size 14. Vic's mom would call her a "mirrorless mutha-fuckah."

I have gone through a transformation brought on by imposed diet. I have not had a cocktail since before the illness. I've lost ten pounds. I have cheekbones again. My jaundiced complexion is camouflaged by a coat of tan purchased from Electric Beach.

The State of California has issued me a fat disability check endorsed by Governor Pete Wilson. He's a living doll. The tax-payers pay for my makeover. I am conscious of California's finan-cial difficulties; I buy clothes from sale rounders. Life Uniform provided by Gap.

I am anxious to debut newfound glamour. I arrange to meet Vic and John for Boys' Night Out. This means NO BOYFRIENDS.

Not a problem for me, but my friends have been coupled for some time. Each has a boyfriend scarcely old enough to drink legally. I chat with the "kids" about Lady Miss Kier and how "hot" Sharon Stone looks.

I have no interest in this type of evening. I want to get laid.

I exit the freeway at West Covina Parkway in my beat-up VW convertible. I know this place. This is where I'm from.

I know this place.

While much of the San Gabriel Valley enjoyed growth and extensive changes during the boom of the '80s, West Covina remains virtually the same: row upon row of simple tract housing, most with stucco façade and flat, rock-laden roofs. The scent of mock orange mixed with carbon monoxide permeates the warm, still air.

As I drive up Sunset Avenue to collect John, I think of Michelle Teal, the girl I dated briefly in high school. I wonder if her folks still live on this street. I wonder what she is doing today.

On the freeway to Los Angeles, John informs me that he has an eight-ball of crystal.

"I was hoping you did."

John is a Club Thang. You can find him in the trendiest bars in town, perched on a stool, desperately clinging to his boyfriend—and his youth. Although I am his junior, John tells new friends that he is two years younger than I. It galls me to think that Grampa Grunge is actually pulling it off. His boyfriend, Gaby, discovered the truth after he and John had been dating for a year. John had unwittingly left his driver's license out after chopping lines with it.

"You should lie about your age too," I am advised. "I told Vic to do the same thing. You guys don't look it." To think of the three of us shaving years off of our ages! The Gay Gabor Sisters. I am Eva. John is definitely Princess Zsa Zsa. Vic is poor Magda.

"You should see Vic now." John puffs out his cheeks when I look over at him. "*El puerco grande.*"

John's diet: a line for breakfast, a line for lunch, and a sensible dinner on Wednesday.

Vic's weight has fluctuated since high school. He has seen diet doctors, popped Dexatrim, and survived on vitamin B_{12} and protein shakes. There once was talk of a tapeworm. His battle with food is constant. I can tell that food is winning when Vic approaches us in the club.

Vic greets me as we embrace.

"Hey, Coif!" He uses the nickname that an ever-changing hairstyle earned for me in high school.

It's good to see old friends.

We make small talk in the bar. We share tidbits of gossip about people we've not seen in a long time. Some I miss. Most I do not. Pointedly, we do not discuss my recent illness.

John hands me a bindle. I disappear with it into a stall in the men's room and tightly roll up a dollar bill. I shake with anticipation. I want to be high. I dip the bill into the bindle, bring it up to my face, and take a healthy snarf of the white crystals. I see red. My eyes water. My face is on fire. Jesus this shit burns.

I rejoin my friends. John has a grin on his sun-drenched face.

"Feeling better, dear?"

I am. Mind-expanding. Free of usual reservations, I chat with strangers. I am witty. I am handsome. I sparkle. I am high.

BATHHOUSE

I stand anxiously in line at The Spa. There are four guys ahead of me. We size each other up. We wonder aloud what is taking so long. I'm curious to see the blond in a towel.

I read the warning: absolutely no drugs or alcohol.

I nervously fumble with the folded paper in my jacket pocket containing the crystal meth that John gave me as I left him and Vic at the club. "Take a little 'Tina' with you," John says, handing me the bindle. It's great to know drug dealers.

Behind a glass partition a man writes down my driver's license information and searches for my name on a computer readout. I am not on the list.

"Room or locker?"

"Locker, please."

The man snorts caustically. Etiquette has no business in a bathhouse.

I am handed a towel with a key and a condom folded in it.

"Locker 587. Your checkout time is 9 A.M."

Once beyond the secured door, I resist the temptation to ape Norma Desmond as I ascend the grand, sweeping staircase. I feel the gazes of men in various states of undress. Some wear the classic towel, some are in Calvin Klein underwear, some wear gym shorts, some are nude.

I strip down in the locker room. The crystal and recent diet have freed me from the usual apprehension about exposing my body. Been working out again; my arms and chest are firm. I see my reflection in smoked mirrors. Highlighted hair shines in dim overhead lights.

In swaddling clothes I pad barefoot through the catacombs. Some of the numbered doors are open. Exposed men sit on the beds in tiny mirrored rooms and manipulate themselves. I am looked at invitingly.

I go into the bathroom and do a quick snarf. I throw the empty paper into the toilet and flush. This is the boost I need.

The drug washes over me. I am adrift in a warm ocean of sensation. The decadence of my surroundings beckons; I am a part of the sinister eroticism.

A rugged, handsome man invites me into his room. His body is exquisite. I tingle at the gentle touch of his large hands. I kneel down and worship him. We share a cigarette when the ritual is complete.

I wander into the video lounge. I hate not having checked into a room. There is no place to hide.

I sit on the crowded bleachers and focus on the monitor. Tanned, beautiful men perform sex acts by a swimming pool. There is not a mole or freckle on any of them. I have not seen such perfectly complected people since *The Lawrence Welk Show* went off the air.

A man behind me moves down and takes a spot at my side. He puts his hand on my thigh. I meet his gaze. There is a connection. We lean into each other, kissing slowly.

"Come back to my room."

I nod and follow the tall man down a long corridor. Inside his room we are passionate, we are tender. We are two people hungry for another's touch. I stay with the man until dawn. As I leave Ted writes his home phone number on a business card.

"Call me."

In the parking lot, I look down at the card. Ted is an accountant at one of the studios in Burbank. I am at once repulsed and impressed. I resent "industry" people.

I think of our few hours together. There was a definite connection. I will call him.

Maybe this time it will work out.

TED

Things are working out for me and Ted. We've been dating for three months. He lives in Santa Monica, a 45-minute commute. Each Friday I shoot up the 405 freeway to see him in his plush apartment with a panoramic view from Malibu to Hollywood. I return to Orange County to work in Mom's office on Monday morning.

Mom practices family law. The stress of divorce and child custody cases is incredible. I have difficulty in comprehending the mountainous paperwork. Mom appreciates my diplomacy in dealing with distraught clients and badgering colleagues.

An angry Doreen Spangler deposits a lovely Chinese vase containing the remains of her soon-to-be ex-father-in-law on my desk. "This is bozo's dad. I ask you, what kind of schmuck would leave his father in his ex-wife's garage on a shelf next to the turpentine?"

I think of a few of my "uncles." I tell Doreen that Nordstrom is having a sale. "A new pair of shoes does wonders for me when I'm in a mood."

I tell these stories to Ted and his friends over dinner. They feign mild interest. For them the only topics of conversation are The Talent and the facts and figures of The Industry. Little else is worth discussing. I am surprised by the arrogance within the accountancy of movie factories. Through budget cuts and audits, accountants drive an industry based solely on money rather than artistic merit.

I am quickly made aware of my inconsequential career. With my obvious lack of education, meager income, and inexpensive shoes, I am scarcely worth talking to.

I'm a toy.

I obligingly answer catty questions about the restaurant trade. When asked at a cocktail party whether or not I've ever done porno, I laugh. I am witty when publicly pressed on the question of whether or not I've ever been paid for sex. Ted does not interfere.

I'm trash.

We listen to pop music. We see bland, formulaic pictures. We shop in the Beverly Center. On Friday nights we gather at La Fabula. The room, crowded with upwardly mobile gay professionals, is dressed uniformly in chambray and khaki. Polo ponies gallop on Nautilus-sculpted chests. We are "straight-acting." It is acceptable to be homosexual as long as we conform to the narrow dictates of Corporate America.

In expensive off-road vehicles we caravan en masse to Palm Springs. Ted and I drink margaritas from paper cups. The cellular phone rings constantly, each party attempting to determine where the other is by location in relation to familiar landmarks.

I had no idea that people live like this.

We arrive in the desert to enjoy a Jeffrey Sanker Easter Extravaganza. Ted and his friends behave like middle-aged frat boys. We buy ecstasy from a man at the pool at the Desert Palm.

I stand in stony silence while Ted and the "boys" check out the meat. Men in G-strings simulate sex acts on a scaffolding. These tea dances are always a scene.

A man gives me the eye. Unnoticed, I slip away to introduce myself. The man offers me a beer. I accept. We saunter away from the crowd, making the usual chatter as we go. We sit on the grass under a shade tree. The man is a teacher from Oregon visiting for the weekend. He is far better-looking than my escort. I am treated with dignity. He listens to what I say. Suddenly I'm human again.

When the man asks me to kiss him, I do.

I don't care.

I feel nothing in this kiss. I am committed to Ted.

I look up to find Ted hovering over us. Unapologetically I introduce Ted to the man. Realizing what he has stumbled into, the man retreats hastily. I wonder if I used him.

Ted sits next to me. We discuss what just happened. I explain why I am offended by his behavior.

"Do you want to be single?"

"I love you," Ted cries. I am taken aback by his tears.

Long time since anyone uttered those three short words to me.

PERSONALS

Suddenly single again, I begin to seek out ways of meeting other HIV-positive men. Disclosure is a difficult process. It would be less risky for me, emotionally, to exclusively date men who share my status.

It would be nice to be able to take a few risks in bed. Sterile sex is boring.

Life is scattered in two different directions. While Ted and I were dating, I saw less of my drug buddies. Since the breakup, John and the gang have provided me with a chemical vacation from the misery that accompanies the sudden split from someone I cared about.

"Do a line honey, you'll feel better."

The drugs do take the edge off. I don't ache at all.

We party from Friday to Sunday, when we turn up at Ripples for Beer Bust. Burnt-out and tweaked, we do not sleep at all on the weekend.

During the week I sober up and hang out with Geoff. I do not tell him about my drug habit.

An elementary-school teacher, Geoff is unlike most of my

other gay friends. He is stable and responsible. He doesn't lie to me. He is not overly conscious of his appearance. He does not enjoy shopping for clothes or changing his hairstyle.

Geoff is concerned for my welfare. He refers to John and Gaby as "them."

I keep my groups of friends separate.

I regularly accompany Geoff to a Wednesday night support group. By midweek I've recuperated. I'm presentable again. Having learned my lesson about saying too much in these groups, I paint a lovely picture of the week when it is my turn to speak.

"Things couldn't be better. I'm doing just great."

Burn the witch.

There is no winning with some people.

After the meeting Geoff and I have dinner at a coffee shop nearby. Amphetamines purged from my system, I again have an appetite.

Geoff says nothing when I order a beer with my meal. He slides a sheet of Xeroxed paper across the tabletop. It is a brochure for *CONNECT!*, an HIV dating magazine.

"It's only 10 bucks for three months."

Geoff would like nothing more than to see me shackled to a relationship.

"It's what you need."

I toy with the idea. I have never tried advertising in a personal column before. What the hell.

A day later, cooped up in John's bedroom, smoking cigarettes and doing lines, we compose my personal ad. I take the game more seriously than John does. It is, after all, my 10 dollars and my life. I want the ad to be reasonably true.

I include my home address as the point of contact. I do not provide my phone number.

For the next few weeks I anxiously watch the mail for my first issue of *CONNECT!*. When it arrives I am shocked to find my ad highlighted on the cover.

PREPPY, 5' 11" BLOND HAIR, BROWN EYES SEEKS SIMILAR FOR DATING AND MORE. I ENJOY THE ARTS, CLASSICAL MUSIC, DINING OUT, AN OCCASIONAL GLASS OF WINE. INTIMACY IS A CONSTANT STRUGGLE FOR ME, YET I YEARN FOR A CLOSE RELATIONSHIP. WILLING TO EXPLORE? PLEASE WRITE...

The ad is headlined CREAM OF THE CROP.

While I have stretched the truth with the frequency and type of alcohol I consume, I have tried to be as honest as possible. The final line is a real stretch for me. There, on the cover of a publication, for all the world to see, I have defined my greatest fear: being intimate.

Out of 17 responses I choose to meet five eligible bachelors.

I endure dinners with each one. Although the men are pleasant and well-mannered, they are the "thriving with HIV" types. I have not yet learned to embrace the disease.

I quickly lose contact with four of the mystery dates.

The fifth, an artist with no tangible means of income, is most intriguing. With curly black hair and hazel eyes framed by thick lashes, Doug is sexy to a fault. He is also a loser. Living life on the edge, Doug appeals to me immensely.

Most importantly, like me, Doug is a crystal fiend.

MEXICO CITY

Geoff and I go to Mexico during his summer hiatus from teaching. Geoff makes this trek annually to visit the family of his deceased boyfriend, Miguel.

The tale of Miguel's death is a dramatic one. Having just been diagnosed with AIDS and suffering from an unnamed illness, Miguel boarded a plane home to tell his family that he was dying. Arriving in Mexico City, Miguel, too ill to walk, was carted through the airport in a wheelchair. Pale and unable to breathe, Miguel was rushed from the airport to a hospital by his sister, Estrella. Miguel died of complications from *Pneumocystis carinii* pneumonia in the waiting room.

It has taken Geoff a long time to shed the guilt of Miguel's death. Before the drama the relationship was floundering.

Drugs being the mainstay of my diet, I am less dedicated to my job in Mom's office. I often blow it off completely. One Tuesday afternoon, burnt-out and still in bed, I lay in my darkened room. Mom stands angrily, hand on hip, a silhouette in the doorway: You're fired.

"I need your office key."

Poor sucker Geoff "loans" me the money for an airline ticket. He feels that a vacation is what I need to help get my shit together. I am not carrying drugs when we depart the United States.

I drink a number of cocktails during the four-hour flight. Assisted by Geoff, I set foot on Mexican soil totally wasted.

"Was a black man flying the plane?"

"No, they were showing *Driving Miss Daisy*."

For the ten-day visit, Estrella's Zona Rosa apartment becomes our home base.

We embark on the usual tourist excursions. With the high level of poverty in Mexico City, I feel at home. The scorched and deserted east side of Wilshire Boulevard resembles Mexico's capital. Why are Angelenos so smugly proud of their urban hell?

We visit a nearby nightclub, Taller. "Means 'auto shop,'" Geoff tells me. The crowd is young. Music pounds in my ears. Every fourth song is in English. Madonna packs the dance floor. Around the room pretty boys form tight, impenetrable circles. Less fortunate souls line the darkened wall. Geoff and I, like most of the other average-looking patrons, mill about the middle of the club.

Fags are fags the world over.

Fluent in *Español*, Geoff makes conversation easily with the boys who approach him. My Spanish, a basic restaurant dialect (*uno limonada, por favor...platos para el pan*), is not enough to buoy a conversation when approached. "No habla *Español*" deters most of my would-be suitors. As always I stand alone in the crowd, my difference this time defined by language. Watching. Thinking. Drinking.

"Do you have a cigarette?" A man interrupts my musings.

"I don't smoke," I lie.

"I don't either."

We laugh. The professor from the University of Mexico City

used a clichéd opening line to attract my attention. My attention is undivided for the rest of the trip.

Culturally aware, Raul instructs me on the finer aspects of Mexico City. Architecture is pointed out and explained. We visit the Palacio de las Bellas Artes and the Museum of History. At the Museum of Modern Art, we talk about the lives of Frida Kahlo and Diego Rivera. I wing it.

The notorious Robert Mapplethorpe exhibit is on display when we visit the museum. I relate why this exhibit is significant in the continuing fight against censorship in the United States. I notice aloud that a few of the questionable photographs have been excised from this showing.

In front of a Mapplethorpe self-portrait, I explain to Raul that the world is now deprived of his talent, his life snuffed out by AIDS.

Raul moves along, leaving me pensive and alone.

The gaunt artist, face ravaged by disease, glowers out of an immense black-and-white photo. The grotesque handle of a cane—a human skull—is thrust into focus. A dead man speaks: *DON'T DIE IN VAIN; DON'T DIE IN VAIN.*

Attracted to Mexico's more relaxed pace and knowing how far my disability stipend will stretch in this city, I agree to extend my visit indefinitely. On the way to the airport, Geoff expresses his delight in my decision. He knows that I am thousands of miles away from a lifestyle that is killing me. We say a hasty curbside farewell at the airport. "Be nice to Raul, he seems like a good guy."

Mom is horrified when I phone asking her to forward my disability checks to Mexico City.

"What about your health care?"

"Fuck it."

I refuse to live life cowering in the face of death.

My living situation with Raul is amiable. I am allowed my space. I am respected. The man adores me.

I do not love him.

As days wear into weeks, the affections from a man who represents a roof over my head become annoying. The closeness is unbearable. I feel claustrophobic. Capricious me.

I pack my suitcase and bolt.

DOUG

I pay the shuttle driver the specified amount plus a few dollars tip. I watch the van pull away, leaving me standing in the drive-way of Mom's house.

The six weeks spent in Mexico were what I needed. I feel strong. Nothing can bring me down. Nothing.

The whir of the garage door opener brings me suddenly back to the reality of Orange County. I am face-to-face with Mom.

"Hi."

"Hi."

Uncomfortable initial greeting out of the way, Mom hops into her car and starts it. I walk alongside the car and poke my head in the window.

"Where're you off to?"

"Court."

"Oh." I smile cheerfully and wave as Mom backs the sports car out of the garage. She does not return my gesture.

Welcome home.

Inside I find Al, the remote control removable from his hand only by surgery, lounging on the daybed in the den.

"Look what the cat dragged in."

I hate him.

Unkempt and obviously hungover, Al has lost his job in Dr. Steadman's office.

"How long you been out of work?"

"Coupla weeks."

"Oh." I pick through the mail. Another state check, thank goodness. I've got $2 in my pocket.

"Some guy named Doug keeps calling." Al does not look away from the screen; *Montel* is very interesting today. "He called again yesterday."

The only number Doug gave was for his pager: "It's the best way to reach me."

I go into my bedroom and open a window. I sense instantly that my things have been rifled through. I page Doug. I want to get out of the house for the day.

Minutes later Al and I answer the phone on the first ring.

"IT'S FOR ME!"

Al hangs on the phone momentarily. Finally, a click.

"What's with that guy?"

"He's just nosy."

"When did you get home?"

"Today."

"Great!" Doug is enthusiastic. It pleases me that SOMEONE is happy to have me back in California.

We arrange a date for the same afternoon. Doug wants me to meet his friends who live nearby, Maureen and Cheryl.

"I'll be by at 4."

Feeling better, I don a pair of sweats and join Al in the den for some early-afternoon TV. I am not shocked to find him holding an open beer can.

"There's more in the fridge, if you want."

What the hell.

After the third Schlitz, animosity toward Al having dissipated, I eagerly devour the latest gossip. Mother has a new boyfriend, she's worried about Gramma, her secretary walked, she loaned my brother $800 to fix the teeth he knocked out falling down a flight of stairs. "He was shit-faced."

Quelle surprise.

3:30 P.M.: I jump in the shower to prepare for my date's arrival.

4:00 P.M.: I rejoin Al in the den.

4:27 P.M.: I open another beer. He's late.

4:43 P.M.: I page Doug.

5:00 P.M.: My page remains unanswered. I'm pissed.

5:35 P.M.: Doug arrives. He offers no explanation. I hold my tongue.

Doug's unshaven face is handsome. His new goatee tickles when we kiss. His mouth tastes good.

"I brought you something." Doug reaches into the pocket of his dingy jeans and produces an Atomic Fireball.

What IS it about guys like this?

I smile broadly. Doug smiles back.

"I brought you something else."

Crystal!

Six drug-free weeks. Back on the merry-go-round.

What the hell.

AUNT KERRY

Miss Adams is angry. The class, hyper at the thought of Christmas and the imminent vacation, has turned the afternoon party into a riot.

"Class! *Class! Take your seats! CLASS!*" Miss Adams slams a yardstick on the desk. It cracks on the third sharp rap, and splinters fly on the fourth. The students laugh uproariously. Miss Adams is not amused.

Red-faced, the teacher finally gains control over juvenile anarchy by leading one rowdy student to his desk by the ear and forcibly seating him. Miss Adams means business.

"*Now,*" Miss Adams says breathlessly, "you children sit and put your heads down this instant. If I hear so much as a peep from any of you, it will be your ticket to the principal's office."

We scurry to our desks and obey orders.

In all of the excitement, I have neglected to go to the rest room. I raise my hand. "Miss Adams?"

"*What did I tell you?!*"

I cradle my head in my arms. Miss Adams has never spoken to me like that before. A well-mannered student, I am silent until called on. During recess I opt to walk with my teacher monitoring the school yard rather than play with my peers. As teacher's pet I am stunned by the biting tone.

I shift uncomfortably in my seat. O-o-oh! O-o-oh! O-o-oh! I really have to go potty. Maybe I can catch her attention. Peeking up, I see Miss Adams holding a compact at arm's length, adjusting disheveled white hair. Oh, never mind.

I lay my head down and stare at the desktop.

Cramps. Ouch. I really have to go. Maybe just one little trickle—a drop. Surely no one will notice a stain in my underwear. Just one drop.

A bit of wisdom for my fellow students: One drop is never enough.

Corduroys soaked through, I sit in a puddle of urine. If I sit quietly and pretend not to notice, no one else will either. Warm liquid begins to cool on my legs. Don't say a word.

"E-e-euw!"

Busted by the resident paste-eater. "Miss Adams, *look!*"

The class begins to giggle. I close my eyes and burrow deeper into the crook of my arm. I hate that fat boy.

The laughter is unbearable. I can't look up. I can't move.

A warm hand touches the exposed nape of my neck. Breath of violet cachou caresses my ear. "Come with me."

Keeping my head on the desk, I cast an ashamed eye on the teacher standing over me. Miss Adams smiles. "You'll be OK. Come on now."

Scooping me out of the chair, Miss Adams leads me from the classroom. Kids laugh.

"Ha ha, potty boy!"

The teacher turns on her heel and glares at the mocking mass. I hide in the folds of a shirtwaist dress.

"STOP THIS INSTANT! PUT YOUR HEADS DOWN."

Silence.

Miss Adams leads me to the administration building. I walk with my head bowed, drenched trousers the mark of my crime.

"Why didn't you say something?"

"I tried."

Miss Adams stops walking. I look to her for an explanation. She returns my gaze and opens her mouth to speak. No words come out. The teacher turns her head, staring thoughtfully down the hallway then back at me again. A liver-spotted hand reaches for mine, enfolding my fist in hers. "Come on."

We enter the school office. The secretary wheels away from her typewriter and smiles as I walk in. "Looks like we had an accident."

"A little one." Miss Adams glances at me. "Would you have his mother bring a change of clothes down?"

I tug Miss Adams's arm. "Oh, please! Don't call my mother."

"We must."

The secretary places glasses hanging from a chain around her neck onto her nose and searches for the file with my phone number in it. Miss Adams shows me to the faculty rest room.

"You stay in here until your mom arrives with a change of clothes."

The heavy wooden door closes. I put the seat down and sit on the toilet. What will Mom say? She doesn't like to have her day interrupted. I wish I could sit in here until my clothes dry. What will happen when Dad finds out? I'm in big trouble.

Embracing myself, I rock back and forth. Why did this happen? I'm gonna get punished for sure.

I sit listening to the whir of the fan in the ceiling, anticipating the dreadful outcome of this humiliating situation.

Finally, a knock. "Your Aunt Kerry is here."

Aunt Kerry! She's here on vacation! This is too good to be true. I crack open the door and peer out.

"Hi, sweetheart."

It IS true. I open the door and reach for clean jeans and underwear. I look at Aunt Kerry. The long minutes of anxiety well up in my eyes. I begin to sob.

Pushing the door open, Aunt Kerry sits me down and removes the soiled clothing. Naked from waist to toes, tears fall to the top of my thighs, then to the floor.

"I thought you'd be Mom."

"She's not home. Did you think you'd be in trouble?"

I bite my lip. Aunt Kerry cups her hand under my chin. She raises my face to hers. Serious eyes look into me.

"You thought you'd be in trouble, huh?"

Shoulders heave. I nod. Aunt Kerry's brow darkens.

"Now you listen to me. Your parents are young. They don't know what they're doing. They're mean to you. You must try to understand. Remember: You are just a little boy. It's not your fault."

I stare at the floor.

"Look at me. Now, what did I just say?"

I can't say it.

"What did I say?"

"I'm a little boy it's not my fault." I've said it. I don't believe it.

"That's right. Now put on your pants and I'll take you home."

We walk in the sunshine. A yellow school bus crosses our path. We stop and wait for it to pass. Without looking down my Aunt says, "This will be our secret."

Crossing the parking lot, I think: *AUNT KERRY IS MAGIC*.

DOUG

It's been four days since I last spoke with Doug. I've grown accustomed to speaking to him on the phone daily. This is the longest absence from Doug I've endured since my unexpected return from Mexico. Countless pages have gone unanswered.

It's happening again.

On the phone I complain about the situation to John, who gives me the usual advice. "Get over it. Come over and we'll do some Tina."

I'm less interested in wearing my misery as garishly as a faux Chanel suit than I am in getting high. To the gang a person's downfall is fodder for gossip and gloating rather than reason for sympathy and understanding. I will see them when I am able to more effectively mask what's really going on.

I'm getting the Brush-off.

On the fifth day, defeated and tired of hopefully answering the damned phone each time it rings, I withdraw to my chamber and crawl into bed. Safety. With a bottle of scotch and some marijuana, I will suffer in silence.

On the seventh day Al, whom I've seen only in passing on the way to the rest room, knocks on my door. "Are you OK?"

"I'm fine, really. Please go away." I have Camille-itis.

Al lingers beyond the locked door. "Are you hungry?"

Ignore him. Eventually, the pound-pound-pound of Al's feet on the floor as he walks away.

Mom never knocks. She never did.

Late that afternoon, low on liquid sustenance, I put on a hat and sunglasses and make a quick dash to Safeway. Inside the store I keep sunglasses on, head lowered. I do not make eye contact with other shoppers.

They know.

My public solitude is interrupted whilst surveying the Hostess display.

"Hey!" It's Doug's friend Cheryl.

"Hey."

"You look like shit."

In the five weeks I've known her, it's become apparent that brutal honesty is one of Cheryl's better qualities.

"You buyin' some Ho-Hos?"

I laugh. It feels good. I refrain from asking the obvious.

"We've been calling you."

"I haven't been around."

Cheryl examines me more closely. I feel naked under her scrutiny. "Maureen is making some dinner. You wanna come over? Have some beers and eat?"

I could use a home-cooked meal. I would, naturally, love a beer. I accept the invitation.

A couple, Maureen and Cheryl have lived together for three years in a pink-and-turquoise beach shack in the neighborhood. Sharing a warped sense of humor and alcoholic tendencies has made us three virtually inseparable since Doug introduced us. I often visit alone, when Doug is incommunicado.

I leave my car in the Safeway parking lot and climb into Cheryl's truck.

"P-e-e-e-yoo! You need a bath."

"Fuck you, bitch."

Laughing, we pull up to "Pee Wee's Playhouse." Maureen putters about the front yard.

"Hey Mo—look who I found!"

I wave goofily. Maureen pushes spectacles up the bridge of her nose with an index finger.

"Where've you been, Boy?"

"Around."

Maureen walks over to take a closer look. "On a bender, huh?"

"Uh-huh." Secret out in the open, I nod my head.

"You wanna take a shower? I've got some sweats you can put on."

"OK."

I follow the girls into the house. In the bathroom Cheryl hands me a folded towel. Bringing it up to my face, I inhale the fresh fragrance of fabric softener.

"You want a razor?"

"OK."

The hot spray of the shower is as satisfying as the mothering of my two new friends.

Presentable, I rejoin the girls for the evening. Unable to shake the situation with Doug, I am detached from the joviality, unusually quiet.

At night's end, after Maureen excuses herself, I finally ask Cheryl the question that has been on my mind for a week. "Have you talked to Doug?"

Cheryl looks down at the bottle of Henry Weinhardt's in her

hand then up at the TV screen. After a long pause: "Boy, there's something you should know…"

I know it. I'm not stupid. I know what she's going to say.

"Doug lives with someone."

DANGER, WILL ROBINSON, DANGER.

I stare at Ted Koppel. I'm not stupid. That's why the pager number. I get it. I knew it all along. That fucker is a piece of shit.

"They're on vacation in San Diego."

I look back at Cheryl. Funny. I've gone numb.

"Are you OK?"

"I'll be all right."

I'm disgusted with myself. I chose to be blind to the situation: the rendezvous during weekdays, no contact on weekends. I've been a fool.

"You wanna stay over?"

I lie between clean sheets on the bed in the guest room, imagining Doug's comeuppance. I think of the tender words and volatile bodily fluids we've exchanged. What fun! Partying! Clubbing! I think of our dreams of building a life together, of our common struggle with disease. I think of those goddamned hazel eyes of his.

That bastard.

Wait until I hear from him, that piece of shit—*just wait*.

ARTSY-CRAFTSY

I dab the paintbrush into a pot of green watercolor and ginger-ly add a few more leaves to a tree in the foreground. Done.

Clacking high heels echo through the classroom. Mrs. Johnson slowly meanders up the aisle toward my desk in the rear.

"What have we here?" asks the district art teacher.

"Mountains," I reply in a tiny voice.

"Very nice. Someday you're going to be an artist."

An *artist!*

I like Mrs. Johnson. She visits our class every two weeks. I hang on to her every word about American art. I am fascinated by the color wheel. Blue and yellow mixed together makes green.

Proudly I paint my name in the lower right-hand corner of the manila paper. Mrs. Johnson slides the painting across the wooden desktop for closer inspection. "Your mama is going to be very proud of this."

I look up into cat-eye glasses. Rhinestones sparkle.

"Do you really think so?"

"Oh, yes! This is quite lovely."

The teacher moves slowly down the row of desks toward the

front of the classroom. She pulls the sweater hanging from her shoulders closer to her throat. "Very good...Nice...Uh-huh..." Cursory words for my fellow students. I am proud that Mrs. Johnson has spent more time with me than anyone else.

I'm going to be an artist!

I run home from school excited to tell Mom about what I want to do when I grow up. An artist! That's me! I'm going to be an artist.

A strange car is parked in the driveway. Company. Hooray! More people to share the news with.

"Mom guess what! Mrs. Johnson says I'm going to be an ARTIST." I proudly present the damp picture.

"Oh, honey, it's wet. Take it out of here. Go hang it on the refrigerator." Mom snickers and looks at the Lady on the sofa. "Kids," she says, shaking her head.

I hang my masterpiece with the magnet securing a grocery list to the metal door. Leaning against the sink, I admire the colorful painting. AN ARTIST.

I walk into the living room and quietly sit in the rocking chair. The Lady smudges red gook on Mom's cheeks. Fascinating. Just like finger paints. "O-o-ooh. Pre-e-etty."

Mom swivels her shoulders around. Her head snaps into position as she fixes me with The Look. "What are you doing in here? You know what you're supposed to be doing. March your ass into that bedroom and put your play clothes on."

The Lady lowers her eyes, exposing wide lids dressed in powder blue. Mom continues to glare.

"Did you hear me?"

I slide my feet to the floor and slowly retreat to my room.

"Kids," Mom repeats angrily.

I hurry and change, not wanting to miss what the Lady is going to do to Mom's face next. She's an artist!

I walk back into the living room, Keds in hand, and sit on the floor in the corner behind Mom. This time I'll be quiet, invisible.

I tie my shoes without looking, transfixed as the Lady paints black lines on closed eyes. Over Mom's shoulder she smiles at me. The Lady is kind. I tiptoe behind the sofa to look at the results.

"*Go outside!*" Mom can see with her eyes closed.

The Lady nods her head. Embarrassed, I push the screen door open and walk out to the front yard. I don't like it out here. I don't know why I'm not allowed to be in the house after school. I'm just bad.

I sit on the low brick wall at the edge of the driveway, waiting for the Lady to come out to her yellow car. She's nice. I wish Mom were like her.

As she leaves, the Lady gives me a miniature bottle of cologne. "This is for you, little boy." She waves as she backs out of the driveway. "Be good!"

I run down the street, holding the treasure above my head. "Thank you! THANK YOU!"

I watch as the car turns into a speck and disappears.

"*Get in here!*" Mom holds the screen door open, waiting for me to walk past. Black lines give The Look a new intensity. "Where'd you put the grocery list?"

"It's under my picture in the kitchen."

I follow Mom to the refrigerator. She yanks the painting down. A magnet rolls across the floor into the dining room. I pick the list up and present it to Mom.

"Do something with this. You know how your Dad feels about artsy-craftsy shit."

I take the painting from Mom's hand, tightly pressing my lips together as I walk down the hall to my room. I plunk down on tile floor and open the bottom drawer of my dresser: the junk drawer. I put the painting on top of my other school projects. Maybe it's not so good after all.

Maybe it's artsy-craftsy shit.

DR. STEADMAN

I have taken a part-time job in Dr. Steadman's office. It is not the position vacant after Al's dismissal. The secretary post is now held by Babs McGuire.

I work from 4 to 9 P.M. I answer phones. I read *People*. I act as a guard. It is in the evening that Dr. Steadman sees her most dangerous patient, file D47. D47 suffers from Multiple Personality Disorder (MPD), as does S29. This job is weird.

Doug calls, finally.

"Good evening...Dr. Steadman and Associates."

"Hi."

WHAT I WANT TO SAY: *You piece of shit! You have fucking nerve calling me here! (CLICK!)*

WHAT I DO SAY: Long time, no see.

HE SAYS: Sorry I haven't called.

I WANT TO SAY: Yeah, right. (CLICK!)

I DO SAY: I understand.

HE SAYS: Can I come by and pick up my CDs?

WANT TO SAY (THE TRUTH): *Yeah, you can pick 'em up at Moby Disc. I hocked 'em to repay the 20 bucks you owe me.*

(CLICK!)

DO SAY (A LIE): Gee whiz, I was gonna return them to you, but I left them in my car and they melted. Sorry.

Before hanging up I tell Doug that I'd go out with him if he were single.

I sit festering as D47 enters the office, dragged in by her seeing-eye dog.

One of her many personalities is sighted.

"Hello!" I am cheery in spite of the fact that I'm angry and that this woman is scary.

D47's file is a great read. It contains the tales of sordid sexual abuse by her father, of 27 alter egos inhabiting her body, of her subsequent blinding in an explosion while cooking illegal drugs, and finally of her suspected murder of a disabled roommate in a mysterious fire. Imagine D47 and her throng of personalities, torch in hand, creeping around a burning house as the wheelchair-bound man screams, terrorized within. His charred remains were unidentifiable.

Can she see me now?

"Can I have a cup of coffee?"

This is my cue to put down the magazine and fix Miss Thing a cup of coffee complete with "extra Cremora and five packs of sugar." I watch as D47 snatches the Styrofoam cup from my outstretched hand. Blind? My ass.

I return to my desk and hide behind a tall partition. I crouch down nervously as Dr. Steadman leads Patient S29 from the inner office. I can tell that an alter ego, Patrick, is inhabiting the patient's body. Patrick, a male of about 23, is in control of the woman's 37-year-old frame. S29 swaggers out of the office past me.

I've reluctantly accepted MPD as a reality. I address alter egos by name if I recognize them. "Good night, Patrick."

Dr. Steadman nervously calls me into her office. "Can *she* see today?"

"I don't know." Sighted days are typically frightening. It is not uncommon to call the police for assistance. "She took the coffee cup from my hand without prompting, if that's any help."

"Shit." Dr. Steadman welcomes the patient into her office. She gives me a look as if to say "Help me" and closes the door.

Alone at last, I draw the blinds and lock the front door. I open the top drawer of my desk and remove an envelope containing keys to the file cabinets behind me. I unlock the file cabinet containing Xanax samples that the nice drug company rep left with the doctor. Opening the bottom drawer, I spy a forbidden booty of pharmaceuticals.

AL WAS FIRED FOR STEALING DRUGS.

I don't care.

THEY'RE HERE

My friends in Miss Peterson's third-grade class are Mark and Becky. We are all mutually disliked by our classmates. Mark is Japanese and loves science fiction. Becky is cursed with red hair and big orange freckles. I am a sissy. We are three freaks, drawn together by our differences.

We ignore the witless taunts of our classmates. Mark has fewer problems than I or Becky; his mother is the nurse's aide. I am impervious to most everything, due to my rigorous training at home. Becky cries easily.

"Don't cry, Becky," I tell her. "They *want* to see you cry."

Truth is, seeing her cry is more than I can bear. What to say? I stand stiffly aside as tears glide down her cheeks.

"Your glasses are fogging up."

She laughs.

We walk to the end of the school yard. Refuge. We lean, our backs against the chain-link fence, gently bouncing in unison. We bounce in silence until the bell calls us back to the classroom.

It's Sci-fi Week on the 3:30 Movie. Mark invites me over to watch *The War of the Worlds*.

"It's real good," he emphasizes.

I'm skeptical. I've spent many afternoons at the Hayakawa residence watching Godzilla movies. I prefer Doris Day, but I'd rather kill a couple of hours at his house than go home. Besides, I know the food's good. Mrs. Hayakawa always has those pink-and-white frosted animal cookies. Real bologna too.

We lay on the floor bellies-down, munching on snacks, the crumbs disappearing into shag carpeting. I watch in horror as Martians land in the Puente Hills. I imagine the Puente Hills Mall inhabited by suction-cup fingered creatures. I am relieved when, at the film's end, Martians are killed by common bacteria.

Mark tells me that Martians are real. "They call 'em UFOs."

In line at the supermarket, the tabloids tout Liz and Dick's divorce, drunken Rita Hayworth, and UFO sightings.

They're real.

When Liz and Dick remarry, people are still seeing UFOs.

They're real.

At night Martians come into my room and gruffly push my legs wide open.

They're real.

One warm summer evening as twilight fades from orange to indigo, I see the spinning, flashing lights. I stare for a moment as lights drift erratically across the horizon. This is no airplane.

I stand frozen on the front lawn. H.G. Wells's grim prophecy is about to come true: The world is under siege! Freeing myself from terror's grasp, I run into the house. I slam the aluminum screen door. My parents look with raised eyebrows.

I want to speak but my throat is tight. My heart pounds in my head. I force the words out:

"They're here!"

"Who?"

"THEY'RE here!"

"WHO'S here?!"

"THEY'RE HERE!" I shriek, rigidly pointing outside.

Dad jumps from his recliner, grabs a baseball bat from the coat closet, pushes past me, and steps onto the front porch. A macramé owl and the rest of my family stare ring-eyed.

I am angrily called to the front lawn.

"Who the hell is here?"

I look up at the flashing lights. I can see now that they are suspended by a big silver balloon.

"Jesus Christ! That's the Goodyear blimp. What did you think it was?"

"Martians."

Dad returns to the house and loudly announces that I am afraid of a blimp. There is much laughter.

I lie down on the cool grass and stare up at the sky.

I know they're real. I know they are.

HALLOWEEN

I am trembling too hard to apply the liquid eyeliner without smearing it. I don't want to look like Joey Heatherton tonight.

I call John into the bathroom to help me out. We were in cosmetology school together. Drugs or no drugs, John's hand never shakes.

I am preparing to parade down Santa Monica Boulevard with my drug buddies. I am the only transvestite in the entourage.

After applying liner to the top lid of each eye, John holds me at arm's length to scrutinize the effect. Both eyes must be even.

"Your pupils are b-i-i-ig, Miss Thang."

In the mirror I adjust a cheap blonde wig. My god, I look like Margo Perot.

I step out of the bathroom to make my grand entrance. I wear a cream-colored silk chemise with rhinestone spaghetti straps. It is a dress I designed for Mom's last wedding. Vic presents a cocktail. John cuts a line. Gaby lights my cigarette. Doors are opened for me. Preston helps me into the car. Life is easy when you wear long gloves. Fags know how to treat a lady.

We promenade down Santa Monica Boulevard. I have done

too much crystal; I feel noidy. I need a drink to come down a bit. We stop at Mother Lode, Rage, and Trunks. I look marvelous with a highball in my hand.

The Boulevard is a spectacle. Throngs of people crowd the street. Spectators outnumber drag queens 5 to 1. Along the way I chat with my sisters.

"Honey, who did your dress?"

"It's a Mackie."

"Bob Mackie?"

"No, Miss Girl, Mackie Rosen of Detroit!"

At a teller machine I spy Ted's best friend, Chris.

"How you doin', Chris?" I purr into his ear from behind.

"Uh, fine?"

Chris doesn't recognize me. I slink away.

I haven't seen Ted since August. After dating for four months, I have not disclosed my HIV status. Ted wants to get tested together. I repeat the futile process. I'm at a loss for a better way to discuss the situation. I am hopeful that, after having known me for a while, Ted will be able to accept me for myself and overlook my glaring imperfection. He does not.

I see Ted a few days after we receive opposing test results. It's final. He is unable to live with my truth. I am unable to live with my lie.

"It's you!" Chris has finished his transaction and run to catch up. "At first I wasn't sure who it was."

I am happy to see Chris. "How are you?"

"Good. I've missed you." I am surprised by Chris's candor. He seems sincere.

Chris invites me behind a hardware store to get stoned. Chris lives grandly with an executive from Paramount. He drives a Mercedes and dresses expensively. He has accepted his toy status easily. Chris has always treated me in a friendly manner.

"I told Ted he was stupid."

I accept the wooden pipe from Chris's outstretched hand.

"How is Ted?" I don't want to know. I ask out of politeness.

"He's in Italy now. It's really too bad about you guys."

Ted's in Europe. I'm in a dress. There is no God.

"How are you doing?"

My answer is a lie. "Great!"

I proceed to skew the truth about what I've been doing for the past few months. Mexico City is the highlight of my conversation. I do not reveal that I have been regularly using crystal since the breakup. I do not divulge the fact that I hold membership cards for most of the sex clubs in town. I don't talk about the early mornings spent at after-hours parties or at The Sketch Pad.

I conceal the fact that I am unraveling at being unwanted. Partying is the glue that holds me together. Drugs give me something to look forward to, something to live for. I merely breathe without them.

At the close of the conversation with Chris, I take a pen from my beaded handbag. I jot down my phone number. We never speak again.

GOSSIP

"What's up with Dr. Steadman and Her?"

Suspiciously I examine Babs's face. I often stop in the office a bit early to chat with my coworker before she leaves to pick up her kids from school. We've never gossiped like this before. "I've noticed it too."

Dr. Steadman has developed an interest in Patient S29 that breaches the Psychiatric Code of Ethics. Weekly hourlong sessions have been extended to two-hour appointments twice a week.

"The doctor doesn't charge Her anymore."

"Interesting."

Babs looks at me from beneath a raised eyebrow. I purse my lips and return her knowing glance.

"I don't think they do much talking in those two hours." Normally I can hear muffled conversation through the heavy wooden door during the doctor's appointments. I hear nothing during S29's visits.

"The doctor draws the blinds before She comes in."

The Levelors remain open at all times.

"You should see the doctor's hair when She leaves." I remove the baseball cap and vigorously muss my hair.

"*Really?!*"

"I wouldn't kid you, doll."

Suddenly the door to the inner office opens. We stop our conversation and watch guiltily as Dr. Steadman copies a document on the Xerox machine. I replace my cap.

"You're here early."

"Just stopped in to say hi to Babs." I affect a broad, cheesy grin.

We chortle softly when the doctor returns to her office closing the door behind her. "Whew! That was close."

I walk over and pour some coffee into a personalized Hollywood mug. Stirring out lumps of Cremora, I walk back to the desk that Babs occupies. The moment is serious. "I can't believe that Dr. Steadman would jeopardize her career like this."

"This isn't the first time." Babs leans forward to let me in on a secret. "She's been investigated by The Board before."

"Really?" Interesting. So. Dr. Steadman lives life on the edge. I take a sip from my cup. "I hear that the patient is in crisis."

"That's no reason for her to stay overnight at Her house."

I lower myself into a padded office chair. Seated, I wheel to the edge of Babs's desk. "It's unethical, whether they're sleeping together or not."

"She could lose her license."

I smirk at Babs. A devilish thought has crossed my mind. "How many personalities does She have?"

"Nine, I think."

Arms extended, I rise, possessed by Mary Wells.

"*I've got nine lovers and I ain't ashamed /*
Nine lovers, and I love them all the same..."

Babs joins in.

"Let me tell you 'bout my first love-er-er…"

Giddy with fiendish delight, we sing of the alter egos. Impromptu lyrics of Patrick, 23; The Captain, or T.C., the leader; the children Deidre, 12, and Dede, 4; and of Deanna, who acts as the alters' secretary, before losing count.

"Do we count Dr. Steadman's husband?"

"That's *ten!*"

We laugh hysterically. I clutch my stomach. Babs wipes smeared makeup from beneath her eyes. Calm again, she looks at me, perplexed. "What about Mr. Steadman? If the doctor's married, she can't be a lesbian, can she?"

"Hmph."

REVELATION

The woman is crazy.

Breaking away from Dr. Steadman's intent gaze, I take a tortilla chip from the red plastic basket and dip into ketchupy salsa. This is probably the worst Mexican restaurant in all of Southern California.

"Now let me get this straight: You're in love with Patrick, but not the patient herself."

"Right." Dr. Steadman continues to stare, searching for the reaction I will not give her. Agitated, she tears little pieces from a damp cocktail napkin with her thumb and index finger.

She's lost it, poor dear. It's the only explanation. How can she be in love with an alter ego? I hide momentarily behind the wide mouth of a margarita glass. I quaff it in a swallow.

"I think I'll need another."

The doctor laughs and orders two more from the salty waitress.

"Make mine a double." What the hell. She's paying.

"Are you telling me that you're gay?"

"Well, not exactly."

"Not exactly?" What? I hope she doesn't start in with that

bisexual drivel.

"I consider myself bisexual."

The waitress approaches the table with our drinks, halting any comment from me. We sit in strained silence until she leaves.

Fiftyish, the waitress is pitiable in a uniform designed for a girl years younger. Rawhide shoulders protrude out above a ruffled sleeveless bodice. Judging by the 'do she hasn't seen a fashion magazine since Carter was in office. Varicose veins pop through thick panty hose as she wearily meanders away from the table. Tough life.

I look to the ridiculous creature sharing my table and take a healthy gulp of frozen libation. I drift in and out of myself as Dr. Steadman gives the details of taboo relations with a distressed patient. The doctor repeatedly points out that she is having an affair with a male alter-ego.

"I don't love the whole system, only Patrick. They are all separate entities of the same body. Patrick is the romantic one."

"Ah." None of what Dr. Steadman says is making sense to me. The "male" inhabits a body equipped with female plumbing. Either this saga is beyond my realm of comprehension or the doctor is delusional. Wait till I tell Babs!

A third margarita gives me the courage to ask: "What about your husband?"

"I'm getting a divorce." Dr. Steadman is matter-of-fact. I look deeply into the eyes of my friend, the human wallet. Emptiness. "I'm going to have your mom handle the divorce. I've made an appointment to see her tomorrow."

Imagine how Mom will react to this story! The anticipation is *too* delicious.

Before stepping out of Dr. Steadman's car onto the pavement in front of my house, I place a comforting hand on the pudgy arm clutching the stick shift. "What about the Code of Ethics?"

Dr. Steadman smiles stupidly. "I don't care. I'm in love."

I carry the last statement into the darkened house.

Flipping on the kitchen light, I find the disastrous remains of a dinner party. Plates and cooking utensils pour over the sink. The counter is covered with an array of glasses and bottles.

I fill a plastic tumbler with tap water and turn off the lights before walking to my room. A rectangle of light glows from beneath Mom's door. I hear the moans of Mom's date.

Oh honey...Oh honey...Oh honey...Oh honey...

Lying in bed, I imagine parents having sex. Disgusting. I pull the pillow tightly over my ears. I can still hear.

Oh honey...Oh honey...Oh honey...

I put a CD in the stereo and adjust the volume to blaring. Soon the house is consumed by Wagner's *Ride of the Valkyries*.

It tickles me when Mom pounds on the common wall.

"Turn that shit DOWN!"

I pull the covers up to my chin, snickering with glee. She ain't heard nothin' yet.

CHRISTMAS

The Carol of the Bells plays over the Muzak system.

DRINK like a fish
YOU got your wish
O what a dish
TASTy delish
merrymerrymerrymerry christmas

What the hell ARE the words to this song?

I've had it. I drag over to a bench and sit. Why do I always wait until the last minute to do my Christmas shopping? I am not into it this year. Not remotely. Not even.

I sit transparent, watching frantic shoppers. Men wander bewildered through the crowd. Mothers push strollers aggressively, a sort of battering ram. *Gotta get done before Junior wakes up.* Not a bad idea. For a moment I understand the use of infants.

"My goodness, it's crazy here!" A frail elderly lady sits down on the bench beside me. I smile and scoot aside.

"Did you find a parking spot?"

"I didn't take a chance. I left my car with the valet."

The lady is impressed. I do not tell her that the young man laughed as he opened the door of the jalopy.

"All this madness makes you almost want to hate Christmas."

I laugh good-naturedly and nod in agreement. How right she is. I do hate Christmas. I humbly suggest that we remove those scraps of paper marked DECEMBER from our Filofaxes and toss them into a waste receptacle.

"I wonder if I can get a cocktail around here?"

The lady raises a penciled eyebrow. "It's kinda early in the day to be drinkin'."

"I could use a little yuletide cheer."

The ancient mask relaxes into a softer, more understanding look. Maternal. Pitying. Youth in the crone's eyes. We know each other. Where are her lips in relation to the lipstick?

"I think there's a bar in that AY-talian restaurant upstairs."

I mutter "Merry Christmas" and retreat. It's the fastest I've moved all day.

I am Man on a Martini Mission.

The restaurant lounge is separate from the dining area. Thank god. A haven from puritans and children.

Seated at the bar, I guzzle two martinis. I feel warm, relaxed.

The decor is standard mall trattoria. Black-and-white checks on the floor, cheap wood stained an unearthly shade of cordovan, the bar inlaid with dark-green marble. My foot rests on a brass rail. I imagine a Katzenbergian executive, hands extended, thumbs touching, creating a frame, uttering the churlish proclamation: "We'll give 'em a slice of Old New York right here in Orange County. They'll *love* it."

High-theme, corporate style.

A dashing mother/daughter duo enter the lounge and sit on

stools at the bar. They carry shopping bags from Saks, Ann Taylor, Banana Republic, and Williams Sonoma. Old Newport Beach money. Mother is well-preserved. Her page-boy hairstyle has only gotten bigger and blonder over the years. I suspect that she has recently undergone extensive cosmetic surgery. A beautiful matron. The kind of beauty a luxuriant lifestyle affords. Daughter wears a younger variation of the same 'do, today pulled neatly into a bow. She is horsey. Collegiate. Takes after daddy's family—the dollared side.

Mother orders a Tom Collins. Splendid choice! Daughter has a Calistoga water. Surprised?

Mother lifts the tall, narrow glass. She swishes the plastic sword, skewering a bit of lime and maraschino cherry about the opaque liquid. Refreshing! Delicious! An ad for the Gin Advisory Commission.

The women enjoy each other's company. They are great friends. Tow heads tilt forward into each other. Laughter. Love. A relationship.

Christmas is a time to celebrate that which is a singularly human experience: cultivating relationships. Relationship of family. Relationship of friend. Relationship of lover. Trust.

I have a relationship with drugs. Drugs.

Drugs.

I settle the bill. Collecting packages, I return to the reality of the holiday season. I quickly locate a pay phone in use by a Gap poster couple. I wait impatiently as the well-scrubbed parents "check in" with the baby-sitter. First kid. First Christmas. Hurry. Hurry. Hurry.

Finally.

I dial the familiar number using Mom's calling card. What the hell. I wait anxiously as the phone rings.

BE HOME. BE HOME. BE HOME.
At last an answer.
"Hello, John? It's me. Got anything?"

NEW YEAR'S EVE

I stare out of the mirror. I wonder what I did with gel, brush, and blow-dryer to make hair like this. Only on special occasions.

I jump back in the shower and rewash my hair. No gel this time. Use mousse instead.

Another dateless New Year. Great.

I blow-dry my hair using fingers rather than brush. Perhaps a looser style would suit me better? The fog on the mirror begins to dissipate as I preen.

When was the last time I had a date on December 31st? It's been at least five years. Probably Blair. The first man to present me with flowers. My only real relationship. An accountant. Handsome. Charming. Had what they call "background." Breeding. I don't know what he saw in me.

Blair. The first man to say "I Love You." We exchanged rings, vows, moved in together, and made each other miserable for a very long year.

What went wrong? Was it my inability to be truthful? The silly lies about my past and upbringing? Was it my aversion to feelings of closeness? My chronic insecurity? Was it me?

I Love You.

Why didn't I believe him? Wasn't I worth loving? Couldn't I love him back? *Couldn't I?*

I put a tie around my neck. The silken noose. Over once, over twice, through the loop, tighten. There. Most-dressed of the gang. Always am.

I couldn't. I couldn't love him back.

I slide a Carpenters tape into the car stereo. Perfect music for melancholia.

I am the last to arrive at Vic and Marco's house. John greets me enthusiastically. Gaby is saucer-eyed and sweaty, smoking Camel Light after Camel Light. They're already amped up.

"Want a line?"

I roll my eyes, accept the mirror, and snarf.

A familiar tingle begins to rise from the nape of the neck. It peaks at the crown of my head. The sensation is unwelcome tonight. Feeling of anxiety heightened; overwhelming sense of despair.

"Have a drink." Marco shoves a Cape Cod into my hand. He smiles broadly with a glimmer in his eyes. He seems nice. Far too good for Vic. Fatso always scores.

I bum a cigarette from Gaby. Drawing in a long, thoughtful drag, I hold smoke in my lungs for an extended moment. I watch as my friends enjoy the company of their partners. I'm the fifth wheel. A tagalong. Odd man out. Confirmed bachelor. Walker?

We five arrive at Rage shortly before midnight. A $15 cover? For this? I'm not even having a good time.

I move to the rhythm of the music, doing a sort of lazy twist. I just can't rise to the occasion. Mercifully, my friends, preoccupied with themselves and madly in love, do not notice my distraction. The hollow thump of dance music mingles with the empty pounding of my speeding heart.

INVISIBLE.

10...9...8...7...6...5...

Who will I kiss?

4...3...2...1...

Happy New Year?

Ambience: Fellini. The crowd around me sways and attempts to sing the words to "Auld Lang Syne." I don't think anyone, with the exception of the survivors of the S.S. Poseidon, really knows the lyrics to this song. Couples kiss and carry on around me as confetti falls ever so slowly to the ground.

INVISIBLE IN THE CROWD.

Across the dance floor, I lock eyes with a scrawny young boy. Strapped to his face, an orthodontic headgear gleams in an unearthly white light. Sardonic brown eyes bore into me. I feel his sadness. Empty. Lonely. A phantom.

LOVE ME.

Unblinking, the apparition shakes its head and evaporates.

GRIEF

I walk into thick, moist early-morning air. I'm gonna freeze my ass off. The convertible top on the Bug is so holey that I don't even bother to put it up anymore. A 25-minute drive down Pacific Coast Highway in the fog is the last thing I want to do. Perfect day for a funeral.

I drive a few miles and suddenly turn back. I can't do this. I don't want to bury my friend. I can't do this.

I don't believe it. It can't be! This is a mistake, a dream. I reject this truth.

Instinctively I park in front of Cheryl and Mo's house. A haven. Safety. I pound on the door. Please wake up! Wake up god-damn it.

"What's up, Boy?" Mo answers the door in her bathrobe. Her hair is wet.

"You're up, I gather."

"Just gettin' ready for work. Come in and have some coffee." I follow Mo into the kitchen and help myself to the mugs.

"Hello, Boy." Cheryl looks a little bleary this morning. Must have tied one on last night. "What are you all dressed up for?"

"Going to a funeral."

"Anyone I know?"

"Nope." I nervously tug at the hem of my wool blazer. I feel strange. Numb. Dizzy. I hope it will pass.

"Get your coffee and come sit down."

I follow Cheryl into the living room as Mo excuses herself and disappears to prepare for the day. I droop into an armchair and sip from my cup.

"You OK?"

"I'm fine." I look away from Cheryl, losing myself in the fish tank. I feel tense. I've got to get out of here. Cheryl knows me too well. I can't hide my distress.

"You want a toke?"

Thank god! Drugs. I nod. The pot smoking ritual is itself calming. A few minutes later I drift away in sublime distraction.

"Where's the funeral?"

"Laguna Beach. I gotta run."

Back on the highway. What kind of X-ray vision does Cheryl have? It makes me uncomfortable the way she sees beyond the mask. No foolin' her. No sir.

I'm late—as usual.

I hope this isn't one of those laying-in-state funerals. Barbaric. I think of my great-grandmother laid out in lavender at the front of a chapel. A shadow. A heavily made-up geriatric mannequin. How different people look in death. Put my corpse out on the curb on trash day.

I enter the chapel on cat feet. I sit in the back row. I look down at the folded pink Xeroxed paper with Geoff's name and dates printed on the cover. It wasn't so long ago that we shared a platonic bed in Mexico City.

I have a gnawing ache in my gut. It must be the chili cheese fries I had for dinner last night. I KNEW I should have had some Tums before I left the house.

The minister stands eulogizing my friend. I wonder if she even knew Geoff. My friend. Dead.

I'm sick. Probably food poisoning. Great. Just what I need, botulism. I think it's lethal.

Am I grieving? Is this nauseous ache sadness? Am I sad? Can't be. Fucking fast food. If I survive this, I'll never eat at Jose McCoy's again.

Members of the congregation stand individually and make sentimental statements about Geoff. *I remember the time when* and *I like to think of Geoff as a* blah, blah, blah.

"Geoff was a most honorable man. If I ever chose to emulate anyone, it would be Geoffrey Mason."

I lower myself back into the chair. What possessed me? I look down at clenched fists. I want to scream.

I bolt from the chapel and run to my car. Fearful of being hugged and cried on, I leave without offering a few words of condolence to surviving family members. Fuck them.

I drive a few blocks when it happens. The miracle.

A vinegar tear wells up in the corner of the left eye and trickles down my cheek, leaving a white stain in carefully applied bronzer. That bitch at the Clinique counter lied. This shit does run.

DIVORCE

Mom's continuing education has taken precedence in our home. My brothers and I fend for ourselves. We cook and do our own laundry. While cleaning the house I find Dad's gin bottles stashed in unlikely places. The bottle in the toilet stays cool while displacing the water. One less gallon to flush. Dad is ecology-minded.

Throughout the years that Mom is in college, Dad becomes increasingly distant from the family. When Mom announces in my sophomore year that after earning her bachelor's degree she will go on to Law School, Dad withdraws completely. He spends little time at home. When he does he is drunk and abusive. Leading separate lives, Mom and Dad seldom talk anymore. When they do communicate it is loud, violent.

In searching for a reason for the breakdown of the relationship, Dad focuses on the obvious: me. The product of a previous marriage, I am the wedge driven between my parents. I am a constant reminder of the fact that Mom has had a life outside of her marriage to Dad.

The closely guarded information on my adoption by Bud was

brought into the open when I was 11. While nosing through a box of family photos, I discovered a birth certificate:

Name: Daniel Marcus Moyer, Jr.

Mother: Marion Elizabeth Greene Moyer

Father: Daniel James Moyer

The birth date is identical to mine. I recognize Mom's maiden name. I do not recognize the name of the father.

I don't know who this child is.

Days later I tell Aunt Kerry that I believe I have a twin brother.

"Why on *earth* would you think that?"

I produce the incriminating evidence. Aunt Kerry laughs. "No, silly. *This is you!* Don't you know that my brother adopted you?"

I do not. The veil is lifted. I know why I'm different.

I am speechless; shocked.

My aunt searches for something to say to comfort me. "It's no big deal, honey. Lots of kids are adopted. Hell, just look at your mom."

A double whammy.

Privy to the dark secrets, I begin to view my family through the wizened eyes of a sage.

And knowledge is bitter.

I no longer trust my family. They are liars. This father is not my own. He is a fraud.

Dad senses my resentment. We openly hate each other.

Mom handles the situation by withdrawing into her education. She can no longer be responsible for her husband, or her child.

Her distance from the situation at home takes its toll. In the summer between my sophomore and junior year of high school, Mom discovers a strange phone number recurring on the monthly bill.

"Did you call this number?"

We three boys do not recognize the number either.

When questioned about the errant phone number, Dad does not deny the truth. He is having an affair.

This final act of defiance hastens the inevitable. Mom files for a divorce.

On the eve of Dad's departure from our home, Mom, my brothers, and I meet Gramma and Grampa at a nearby Italian restaurant. It is the Greenes' thirty-fourth wedding anniversary.

The six of us sit at a table set for seven. The empty chair is a conspicuous reminder of what is happening at home. Mom tells her parents that the marriage is ending.

Gramma is shocked by the news. "I had no idea."

After a brief recovery Grampa asks, "Why?"

Mom proceeds with the unfortunate tale. She does not address the fact that she and Dad have simply grown apart. "Bud chooses to blame the boy. Obviously, it's not his fault."

With one sentence Mom dispels a truth that I have believed for 16 years.

It's not my fault.

In this moment of realization, a childhood of doubt and fear pits a tender heart. Searing shards of acid in a savage hail of rage.

It's not my fault. And I know it.

In this public place private tears pour down from eyes that witnessed the hatred and cruelty of a man tormented by the ghosts of Himself.

It's not my fault.

I will not cry again.

MARTY FELCHER

There's an insistent knocking at the front door. I'm not going to answer it. Rolling over, I snuggle into the comforter. I feel like shit.

I've been in bed for two weeks. I have no energy. A nagging headache gives me a stupid feeling. Ringing. Buzzing. The thought of food repulses me.

D-i-i-ing Dong! Someone discovered the doorbell. Go away, I'm on drugs! AZT. I'd rather do crystal, but this is supposedly extending my life. Hot damn.

Bang! Bang! Bang! Knocking again. For chrissake. I lunge out of bed and slide open the aluminum-framed window. "Unless you're Cheryl or have a pizza, I suggest you get lost."

"My name is Marty Felcher. I'm here about the ad in CON-NECT!."

CONNECT!? I haven't had an ad in that publication for at LEAST a month. I put on my filthy robe. I haven't done laundry since, well, it's been awhile. Barefoot, I walk downstairs and open the door. A cold wind blows through me.

"Hello."

I'm stunned. Can't speak.

"Can I come in?"

Clutching the robe to my throat, I nod and move aside. I manage a weak smile as Marty floats past.

"Nice place."

"Thank you."

Marty's lips curl into a toothy grin.

I look outside. Is there a hearse parked on the street? Satisfied that one is not, I close the door. I lead the uninvited to the living room and insist he has a seat. In my hostliest voice I manage, "Would you please excuse me?" Without awaiting an answer I turn on my heels and climb the stairs to my bedroom.

The ad distinctly said PLEASE WRITE. OK. So I'm an idiot for putting my home address as a point of contact. John told me so. I never expected anyone to just show up. The temerity!

I pick through laundry piled high on the floor. Something here has to be sort of clean. Sniffing pits and crotches, I finally decide on a rumpled denim shirt and jeans. Who cares? Topping off the ensemble: a saucy baseball cap. I look dreadful. I do a few stretches, bend over, shake my arms out, and descend the stairs. Courage. I walk into the living room with what oomph I can muster.

If he's here, who's keeping the billy goats out of town right now?

Marty watches appreciatively as I sit in a rocking chair at the far end of the room. Not far enough. Oh, to be rocking in Nevada.

"Nice place."

"So you said." I'm bored. Already.

"I'm a restaurant critic."

"How lovely for you."

"What do you do?"

"I'm an actor." When in doubt, lie.

"Well, you certainly look like one." Marty leers. I laugh.

What color is this man's skin? Gray? Beige? Taupe? He's decidedly monochromatic. I wonder if he's ever been draped by a color specialist to determine his season? He must be autumn. Autumn 1917. Perhaps orange would spark up his complexion? Marty's leer gets grinny.

"Have you been in anything recently?"

Who does he sound like?

"Well I, um…YES!"

"Anything I may have seen?"

"Not unless you're a network exec." I find myself inventing a sitcom pilot starring Tyne Daly and the Landers sisters.

"Ann Landers and Dear Abby?"

"Actually, I meant Judy and Audrey."

"Oh?" Marty's perplexed. I really am an actor.

"Maybe you'd like to have dinner with me tonight?"

This voice is SO familiar.

"Thank you, but I'm not feeling well. I just started on AZT."

"Oh, that. You'll get used to it."

"That's what the doctor says."

"It's true. I've been on it for two years. Maybe you need a back rub."

Before I can protest Marty rises from the sofa and drifts to the rear of the rocking chair. Bony digits cut into my shoulders. I don't want to be touched.

"You know, you're a handsome guy…"

That voice! Is it Boris Karloff?

"I could be very good to someone like you…"

Mercedes McCambridge?

"I want to kiss you. I think I will."

Peter Lorre! He sounds like PETER LORRE!

In the wink of a bat's eye, Marty grabs my head and presses icy lips on mine. The undead have no temperature. *Vampire! Don't let him near your throat!*

I turn my head quickly, pushing the gargoyle away. Thin lips curl into a menacing smile. Anne Rice couldn't have conjured up a more gruesome character.

"You know, I'm really not that kind of…"

"I think I'll kiss you again."

Not about to be molested again, I scramble out of the rocker, turn, and make the sign of the cross with my index fingers, holding both hands in front of my face. Marty backs away, frightened. Seizing the moment, I utter the only Latin I know: "E Pluribus Unum."

Marty straightens up. "Are you Catholic?"

"No, an accountant." Lost him. "Kidding. It's AIDS-related dementia. Comes and goes." Nonchalant, I wave my hand.

"Too bad."

That did it. My guest disappears into the twilight only to return four days later. This time I don't let him past the locked front gate.

Ought I have driven a stake through his heart?

POMONA

Fed up with feeling miserable, I stop taking AZT. If this is life, I don't want to live it.

Party!

I call John. I have The Craving. It's been a month since I've seen the gang or had a straw in my nose.

"Coify La Rue!" John is enthusiastic. A sale.

"Hey, doll."

"Where've you been."

"Sick."

Silence. Although John considers me a close friend, one of the inner sanctum, he infrequently calls. He usually phones when I owe him money or if he and Gaby are having problems. I sense his stiffness at my revelation. On to another topic.

"What are you guys up to tonight?"

"Dollar beers at Alibi. Why don't you meet us?"

The usual Friday night happening. We arrange to meet at the club at 11:30.

It's raining. I can't make a 50-mile journey without a top on the car. "Mom, can I use yours?"

"I need it back by 9 tomorrow morning. I have a seminar to go to." Mom knows that my nights out often last all weekend.

"I'll have it back, I promise. Ple-e-eze…"

She tosses me the keys. Eureka!

I feel *quel* hetero in the sports coupe. Stereo thumping, I gun the engine at stoplights. I feel kind of important. I do 80 on the highway. Testosterone courses through my veins. What a stud I am.

A "chick" in an elevated truck flirts with me. I flirt back. Day-Glo-pink lipstick blows kisses. Stiff shoulder-length hair has been processed countless times. How does she comb that nest out when it's wet?

I park in the dirt lot across from the club. Stupid to wear suede shoes in the rain. I trudge through mud.

Beautiful Pomona. Alibi East is located in a less-than-desirable district. Not that any of Pomona is desirable, but there is reason to be afraid for your life in this neighborhood. Local gossip recalls gunshots and fag bashings. I would prefer not to die on the streets in this town.

Alibi East. Always popular on Friday. I assume a position at the end of the line in front of the club. I SHOULD be shot. Better than dying of embarrassment. No paparazzi around. There is a God.

The doorman cards me. What a pal. I pay the $2 cover and enter the club. Always an interesting evening? This place must accept food stamps.

I push my way through the crowd, furtively searching for any member of the gang. No sign of John. FUCK! I'm ready for a line.

"Dearest heart!"

Wheeling around, I come face-to-face with Bart, one of Gaby's friends. Very grand. Barrymore-esque. Tells people he lives on an estate in posh San Marino. Horses. Swinging gates. Wealthy grandparents. I was shocked to discover the truth. He lives around the corner from a *groceria* in El Monte. Hardly a life of luxury. The "stables" consist of a solitary goat tied to chain-link fence.

"Bartina!" I humor him.

"I've *got* to talk to you."

"Oh?"

"I'm getting tested."

Big shit. Since when did I become HIV counselor to the stars? For some reason, after my status hit the streets, I have been forced to listen and give advice to people toying with the idea of getting tested.

"Don't do it unless you're ready to accept responsibility for the results. The worst thing I ever did was get tested." This is my patent retort.

Bart backs off. It's not what he wanted to hear. "Have you seen John?"

"Not yet. I was supposed to meet him 45 minutes ago."

The DJ plays a Madonna abomination.

"Gotta dance." Bart bebops away to the dance floor.

Madonna. Yuck. When did the pure pop of that first album decline into the commercial dirge of *Erotica?* My fag brothers keep buying it. "*But she has the talent to reinvent herself,*" they say. Into what? Swine is swine dressed in lace or leather.

I scope the crowd. Not the best place to find a soul mate. Very blue-collary. Warehouse workers. 7-11 personnel. Low-level computer programmers. Miller's Outpost chic. Must have been a sale. How many of these guys have done time?

"Hi, Coif."

"JOHN! Finally."

AFTER HOURS

"Anyways, like I was sayin', we was just settin' there, fixin' tuh wait…"

He lost me.

I look at John and Gaby engaged in a furious game of cards on the coffee table beside me. John doesn't raise an eyebrow. Cards slap down on wood-grained Formica.

The host of the party drones on about nothing in his aggressively bad English. I wonder: When exactly did he drop out of high school. For three hours I have endured the incessant chatter. He quickly runs through a limited repertoire; I have heard the same stories repeatedly. Edgy and bored, I cringe at each slaughtered sentence.

The jerk is generous with beer and drugs. Shut up and listen.

Across the room a group of bitchy young guys sits on bar stools, inhaling laughing gas from a green balloon. All are dressed in MTV-inspired grunge, a look my fossil friend John embraces. Cheap to imitate, requiring little thought and a minimum of personal style, grunge is indicative of the trend toward anti-glamour. Slothwear. Glorified white-trash. Alternative. When did

Alternative become mainstream? If mainstream is alternative, then what is the alternative to mainstream?

I look down at my J. Crew shirt and dungarees. This ensemble has given the bitches plenty of fuel for their brand of cattiness. Throughout the early morning, as The Jerk works my Reserve Nerve (the one reserved for small children and Jehovah's Witnesses), little punks sit looking down from stools, making no effort to socialize and less effort to conceal the fact that they are contemptuously dissing all of us. My manners and mannerisms have been dissected with scant cleverness and zero wit. The refined air that I have affected (leaning forward, legs crossed at the ankle: Jackie Kennedy craning to hear the shah of Iran) is unappreciated by this crowd.

What am I DOING here?

Drugs. The only thing I have in common with these pigs. We all like to get high, the single shred of sameness that I share with these tedious caricatures of Generation X. I am, perhaps, a few years older than they, but I couldn't be like them if I tried. Even the "art" of the wisecrack, an American classic, is lost on these kids. They are the cultureless generation. A frightening vision of what America has become.

Aren't we all?

I excuse myself from the party, walk to the kitchen, crack open a beer, and step onto the back porch. Delicious solitude. I savor the moment. The rain has subsided. Pomona air smells fresh. Crisp. Clean. I draw in the fragrance of wet earth. A rooster crows in the distance. Morning. Soon it will be daylight.

I've got to get Mom's car back. Why did I leave the car in the lot at Alibi? Swift move. If only I had it now.

Bart comes out and lights a cigarette. "What are you doing out here?"

"Collecting my thoughts."

Bart offers a Marlboro. Using a shriveled hand, he fumbles with a lighter, attempting to ignite the cigarette I hold between my lips.

Poor guy. That accident must really have been something. After a night of drinking, the left foot trails along behind the right, dragged down by its own weight. I wonder if he was drunk. Did anyone die?

Realizing how little I do know about him, I lure Bart into a conversation about his family. A fascinating tale unfolds:

The product of an alleged rape, Bart's "retarded" mother was unable to properly care for the boy. A government agency removed the child from the mother's custody and placed him in a series of foster homes. At 11 Bart was allowed to live with his "religious" grandparents in El Monte. A difficult situation for an adolescent struggling with his sexual identity. Still living with his mother's parents, Bart conceals his true nature, inventing girlfriends and fibbing about where he's going at night.

"The thing is, none of this has affected me at all."

My jaw drops open. "You've got to be kidding, Bart. How can you believe that none of this affected what you've grown into? I mean, it's the stuff *Oprah* is made of."

Bart laughs anxiously. The recognition of him is uncomfortable.

"I'm going back inside. See ya in there?"

"In a minute."

Alone in the dawn, I form a new opinion of Bart. I see why the lies. The truth is too damn painful. I get it. Empathy. Compassion. Understanding.

Been there.

LUCY AND ETHEL IN THE RAG BIZ

During my senior year of high school, I win second place in the annual Art Fair. I have fashioned a gown for Lisa Davis to wear to the prom. It is constructed from various Butterick patterns in Mrs. Schwartz's Sewing II class.

Like all teachers in the West Covina Unified School District, Mrs. Schwartz teaches in two departments. She is also my Sex Ed instructor. The Taxpayers Revolt of the late '70s by walrus-like Howard Jarvis makes this doubling up of responsibilities the rule of thumb. Proposition 13 effected the dismantling of a respectable public school system for the greed of individuals, at the expense of their children. Mine is probably the last class to benefit from a decent education at a cost to society.

Mrs. Schwartz remembers Marion Greene. Mom left Edgewood High School in disgrace 17 years earlier.

Vic photographs me for the school newspaper. Holding the original sketch, I stand beside a dress form, gown draped to the floor. A second-place ribbon is secured to the bodice. I am all teeth.

Vic and I work at a newsstand in Westwood on the weekends.

Actually, Vic works, I hang. I am energized by the excitement of Los Angeles. It is only 40 minutes away from home, yet it's a different world compared to the sleepy suburb we commute from.

On the way back to West Covina, we stop at Fiorucci to check out the sale rack. Vic checks out the guys. I check out the guys. Best friends, we have not told each other our hideous truths.

Vic convinces Dave, the owner of the newsstand, to bankroll my couture line. We are granted $10,000.

ETHEL: I dunno, Lucy...
LUCY: For heaven's sake, Ethel, have I ever had a bad idea?
ETHEL: (Hand on hip, nostrils flared) Oh, brother.
LUCY: Never mind that. Draw, girl, draw!

We hire a Guatemalan seamstress to make my fantasy frocks a reality. The collection consists of Adrian knockoffs. During trunk shows potential buyers comment on the movie-star quality of the designs. I pay homage to my model-of-the-moment, Tina Chow, by creating a quasi-Balenciaga gown with a voluminous acetate taffeta skirt. All fabric is purchased at retail prices.

Our business cards, emblazoned with my signature (the company trademark), are embossed. They are printed on gold foil. Trademark cloth labels are manufactured and sewn into each of the lined garments. Vic hires an answering service.

ETHEL: An ANSWERING service?! You've really flipped your hennaed cork this time.
LUCY: Be quiet, Ethel. We'll make it up in sales.
ETHEL: At this rate we'll have to sell each of these things for...
LUCY: Five hundred dollars apiece.

ETHEL: *(incredulous)* You mean *FIVE OH OH?*
LUCY: Uh-huh.
ETHEL: *OH-OH!*

The collection debuts at the monthly meeting of the Christian
Women's Club. They meet every second Tuesday in the Covina
Bowl's Pyramid Room. We receive a standing ovation from a
group of ladies bedecked in Mervyn's fashions. We are aghast at
their dresses; they are appalled by our prices.

LUCY: Not one order?
ETHEL: Not point oh oh.
LUCY: OH-OH!

Vic makes an appointment with the head of Better Dresses at
Neiman Marcus, Beverly Hills. With big black hair and Kabuki
makeup, the Amazonian woman resembles a young Diana
Vreeland.

*(Mary Wickes guests as Betty Barracuda, fashion maven. A young
Barbara Eden enters wearing a wacky Ethel Mertz creation.)*

BETTY: *(motioning to the balloon-like skirt)* What is going on
with *this?*
LUCY: It's a pouf.
BETTY: A pouf?
ETHEL: Yeah, on account it's POUFFED up with air.

(The girls laugh.)

BETTY: *(Unamused)* I see.

In September, our dreams of prosperity in the glamorous world of fashion faltering in bankruptcy, Vic and I enroll in the cosmetology program at Citrus College.

LUCY: WAAAAAAAAA!
ETHEL: WAAAAAAAAA!
FRED: Don't cry, Honeybunch. You've still got the dresses.
RICKY: That's right, you girls still got the dresses. Now don' cry.

(Ricky hugs Lucy. Fred hugs Ethel. The men face away from each other. The girls look over their husbands' shoulders and wink. In close-up Lucy gives the OK sign. The band plays the closing interlude. Fade out.)

THE END.

DRUG TEST

Goddamn Dr. Steadman. If it weren't for her, I wouldn't be here.

These bullshit questions. I answer with the usual panache.

DO YOU SMOKE? Certainly not.

DO YOU DRINK? Moderately.

IF YES, INDICATE HOW MUCH. Moderate amounts. Why tell them I drink constantly? They'll probably be able to tell that by the urinalysis.

HAVE YOU TAKEN ANY PRESCRIPTION DRUGS IN THE LAST 30 DAYS? Now, this one is a toughy. Do they mean prescribed to me? Does someone else's prescription count? Shit. I'll come back.

IF YES, PLEASE LIST MEDICATION BELOW. Great. What would allow me to test dirty? Poppy seeds read as heroin, the one drug I haven't done in the last month, but what could turn up as marijuana? Shit! Maybe it would be best if I didn't list any of the HIV-related meds I'm on. If they can't abide pot smokers, they certainly won't deal with AIDS.

HAVE YOU TAKEN ANY PRESCRIPTION DRUGS IN

THE LAST 30 DAYS? N-O.

Fuck it.

I present the four-page questionnaire to the receptionist. She peruses the bogus answers, tells me to sit, and slides the frosted-glass window shut.

I pick up an outdated *Time* and resume my position on the cold vinyl sofa. This situation is degrading. I'll never pass the drug screening. I need a job! I need my drugs! I'm a waiter, for crying out loud! What do they expect, stable hash slingers? The service industry is notoriously fucked-up. It's the reason I keep going back to it—I'm with my kind.

Goddamned Dr. Steadman. I knew that little affair would explode sooner or later. The object of the doctor's warped affections had a girlfriend of eight years.

"They reported me to The Board," bemoaned the fool. "I have to close the practice down. I'm sorry."

It was all I could do to keep from saying a deserved *I told you so*.

The clinic door opens and a somber parade of orange-vested roadside workers files in. Probably dragged away from pickaxes and trash skewers without warning. I'd definitely be doped-up for that job. Group testing. At least my humiliation is less public.

Who said this was legal? The Reagan administration? And look who gets tested. Nobodies. There's not one senator or judge in here. I say we march all of Congress down to the clinic and let them have a go at it. After you, Mr. Gingrich, *j'insist!*

A woman in a white lab coat calls my name and leads me to the inner office. I am given a hospital gown and left alone to "strip down."

"Can I leave my underwear on?"

"Yes."

Nothing worse than having your ass hang out in public.

My blood pressure, weight, temperature, and height are record-ed.

"Shoe size nine-and-a-half," I cheerfully volunteer. The nurse does not respond. It seems as though her humor was lost after the disastrous results of her last Ogilvy Home Permanent.

"Now breathe."

I blow into a long tube meant to monitor my lung strength or something. I really don't know why I'm doing this.

"Again."

I repeat the process. "Why am I doing this?" I ask as I come up for air.

"No talking. Breathe. Harder!"

She rips the statistical tape from the machine and staples it to my chart. I am then given a back and chest X-ray. All this for a waiter job.

The nurse hands me a plastic cup with a screw top and shows me to the rest room. "The test is semiprivate."

"What does that mean?" I ask, dreading her response.

"You are being watched."

I close the door for reason of instinct rather than privacy. Being shy, I can't pee in a public rest room if it's occupied by another or if I think you can hear rushing waters outside the door. The thought of peering phantom eyes beyond the looking glass is enough to make a bladder retreat to the nether regions. After this ordeal I may never urinate again.

Get over it.

I unscrew the lid and nonchalantly attempt to go about my business. Damn! Not even a drop. I look over my shoulder into the mirror, flash a toothy grin, and shrug my shoulders. Bet Nazi Nurse is getting a laugh over this.

Irritated, I turn the sink's hot-water spigot on—an old trick learned from Mom. Dry. As if anyone could pass water off as a specimen.

Eventually, after singing a few bars of "Raindrops Keep Falling on My Head," I fill the cup. Head held regally high, I exit the bathroom and present a jigger of me to the woman with whom I've been insultingly intimate.

All this for a waiter job.

WAITER

I arrive early for my first shift: training. I wear new black trousers and dress shirt with faux Armani tie. Mom foots the bill for my uniform.

Waiting tables. I had hoped to never serve the masses again. Oh, well. It's a job. My ticket to freedom.

"Gee, you're here bright and early!" A pachyderm introduces herself as she pulls long, feathery hair back into a Scrunchy. Patti in a Scrunchy. What did I expect in a mall restaurant?

"Did you memorize the menu?" Patti asks while preparing a pot of coffee. I nod and smile half-heartedly.

What's to memorize? The cuisine is as commonplace as the drudge that's going to train me: quasi-nouvelle-california-italian-light-eaters fare. Pesto, angel-hair pasta, baby vegetables, buffalo mozzarella. A holdover from the trends of the '80s, prepared by former Denny's short-order cooks. People who eat in malls won't know the difference. I'm sure the folks of Orange County will think this garbage is the cat's pyjamas.

"Did you hear what I said?"

"I wasn't listening, sorry."

Jumbo the waitress scowls and foists a pitcher into my hand. "Water my tables."

There's no dignity when wearing an apron.

I walk onto the "floor" bearing water, a cheshire cat grin stretched across clenched teeth. Three women of Eastern European or Persian descent have recently been seated.

"Vaiter! Are you our vaiter?"

"No. Let me fetch Patti."

The women resume their conversation in a tongue I can't quite identify. Hermes scarves and gold shoes give me the impression that they are probably Persian. Where the hell is Persia, anyway?

"Hud-a hud-a Bennetton, hud-a hud-a Chanel, hud-a hud-a Fendi."

Definitely Farsi, peppered with the international language of retail.

A busboy fusses with a high chair at a table nearby. An infant. Goody. I wish parents would inflict their children on fast-food restaurants exclusively.

"Could we get some crackers for Junior?"

"Absolutely!" I walk to the wait station and prepare a basket of Saltines. For reasons beyond my comprehension, parents insist on allowing these little beasts to not consume crackers as one would expect but to chew and spit them out as a form of entertainment. While a mouthful will keep Junior pacified for a moment, it also creates little mounds of dough sodden with baby spittle which I, the server, am expected to clean up without wretching.

"How's it going?" Patti asks.

"Fine."

"Those for the kid?"

"Uh-huh."

"I'll take them." Patti snatches the basket from my hands and waddles onto the floor. I follow.

"*Tonya!*"

"*Patti!*"

Jumbo drops the crackers at the kid's table and rushes over to hug another gargantuan girl. They jump up and down in each other's arms.

Patti turns to me. "This is my friend Tonya. She comes in almost every day! She works at the Ultima II counter. We were on *pep* squad together!"

The girls giggle.

"I'll have an iced tea," says Tonya.

"Let me," I implore. I've got to get away from these two before I do one of them serious injury. I'm sure they both carry pictures of Michael Damian in their wallets. Probably the sole surviving members of the fan club.

Patti follows me to the wait station as I pour iced tea into a glass. She leans a buxom buttock on the counter and jots an order on a numbered ticket. "Tonya is *so* cool, we've been friends for years! She has the same thing every day: iced tea and cheese-cake."

"Looks like it."

Patti laughs momentarily. Then, clarity. Piggy eyes narrow.

The manager motions to me. "I need to see you in my office."

Patti takes the glass from my hand and purses her lips smugly.

I walk into the office without knocking.

"I can't hire you."

"Why?"

"You failed the drug screening."

"Oh. What'd they find?"

"Pot."

I knew it.

"They just got the results back. I'm sorry."

I am given a crisp $20 bill from the petty-cash drawer and sent on my way.

Freedom eludes me again.

Damn.

TROY

Is he looking at ME?! I glance over my shoulder. The guys behind me seem preoccupied within their closed circle. I look back at the handsome stranger. He is looking!

We continue to do the Cruising Fandango (he looks, I look, don't look, DRINK! I look, he looks, drink drink drink). With blond hair and a coat of tan, this guy is a knockout.

Ripples' Sunday Beer Bust is an institution. Crowded. Stifling. A scene I generally shy away from. I feel like maybe a date is in order. It's time. I had not anticipated this. I think Bohunk is out of my league. Could he really be interested in me?

A man I've known in the biblical sense arrogantly strides over, taking a place at my side. "Hello," he says, smarmily.

"Hi." I turn the corners of my mouth up, a sort of sneer/smile.

"What's your name?" he slurs.

"Don't you remember?"

Bozo's bewildered. Laboriously he searches the annals of his alcohol-soaked memory. "Should I?" He slips an arm around my shoulder.

"Why, YES! We met at an adult bookstore. I'll be SO hurt if

you can't recall."

The arm drops from my shoulder. I look over at the blond, who is intently observing. I wish this drunk would piss off.

"Oh, yeah. I remember. Your hair is different, it's…"

"Blond?"

"Yeah, blond. Uh, nice seeing you." The man staggers away. I remember. A fellow whore. Smells just like he did that first night. Lagerfeld and Budweiser.

The blond is curious, unsure of what has just happened. Let him wonder. I lower my head, peering out from beneath the shock of hair that has fallen above my eyebrows. I flash a calculated smile—the one that implies wholesome innocence.

Got him!

Seizing the moment, Blondie saunters over. A charming grin adorns his face.

"For a minute I thought I was a goner."

I laugh. "I told that guy I was saving this spot for you."

This fib pleases my new friend. He flashes white teeth. Tiny lines crinkle around sparkling eyes. The right age; he must be over 30.

Troy is 36, to be exact. A professional. Owns his own accounting firm. Another bean counter. What is it about CPAs? I seem to be a magnet for them. As if I'm the centerfold for *Accountancy* magazine. They just sniff me out.

"I live in West Hollywood."

He owns! Stability. A catch. "I live in Orange County."

"I have a sister in Irvine. I hardly ever see her. I guess now I have a reason to get out there more often."

Troy flashes that smile again. He seems to be quite taken with me. That's fine; I'm smitten with him. I continue to work my all-American looks to best advantage, smiling and listening with great interest to the standard introductory palaver. He is cute. I still can't get over his apparent interest in me.

"Let's get out of here."

I nod and follow Troy out of the club. Spring air blowing off the water is cool, brisk. A smattering of stars light a violet sky.

"You don't see those too often," I say motioning heavenward. "Not in L.A."

We cross Ocean Boulevard and walk onto the sand. Gentle waves lap at the shoreline. A perfect evening.

"Are you cold?"

I am, but I lie.

Troy puts his hand on the small of my back. I turn and smile. Not a phony Hollywood smile, but one that comes from inside. Warm. Honest. Content.

With one brief kiss glacial bitterness melts away.

It is a perfect evening.

MONDAY

It's amazing what a little romance will do for the spirit. I feel wonderful.

As a matter of fact, I feel SO good. I don't have the usual jitters that accompany a job interview. I breezed through the initial interview with a personnel flunky, betraying nary a flaw in my character. I now wait to meet the Guest Services Manager.

The ad said CONCIERGE. What a title. French! CON-CI-ERGE. Sounds so much better than FOOD-SER-VER.

Adrenaline. Gosh, I feel good.

"I'm Georgeanne Clancy, Guest Services Manager."

Inexpensive chunk jewelry clatters about the wrist I shake vigorously. Faux Chanel gone berserk.

"Pleased to meet you, Georgeanne."

"Please, call me Georgie."

Throughout the interview I am dazzled by Georgie's brazen display of bad taste. Rhinestone hearts dangle from golden bows at each ear. Strand upon strand of metal and plastic beads hang from a thick neck. A low-cut, machine-washable polyester blouse is printed with an array of jewels and belts. That imitation Hermes thing. On sale for $19.95 at an off-color retail outlet. Maybe mail-order? Home Shopping Network? The ampleness of exposed bosom calls to mind the serving wenches of centuries past. A tiny white skirt and matching pumps are far from businesslike.

"I see here that you've been employed as a waiter. How do you think that experience would have prepared you for a career as a concierge?"

Oh, brother. These trite questions. Georgie moves the tip of her tongue about her molars, vainly seeking out that last bit of roast beef left over from lunch. I answer enthusiastically. Bullshit, bullshit, bullshit.

I doubt she's even heard two words I've said. This is a manager on the ladder to a career as a hotel exec?

The Newport Resort is managed by The Hyton Corporation, an international hotel chain. The corporate structure, such as it is, makes it easy for people of this caliber to climb into middle management levels not by merit of their competence but because of an ability to play The Game. Politics. Schmoozing. Boobies. One can only imagine how this tart moved into her position.

My monologue of keywords, catch phrases, and diplomacy is satisfactory.

"You seem like a likely candidate for the position. Let me call my manager and see if he's available. How soon can you start?"

"I'm available now."

"Wonderful!"

Georgie pulls a bauble from an earlobe and brings the phone receiver to her face. "David? It's Georgie. Tee-hee-hee. Now stop! This is business. There's someone here I'd like you to meet."

TUESDAY

"He calls me What?!"

John looks up from the mound of crystal he is fastidiously dividing and forming into rails. "Satan."

I choke on laughter. I'm not sure how to react. Vic and I have fought before, but he has never nicknamed me Satan! REALLY! I would have preferred Lucifer.

"You mean he's still pissed over what I told Marco?"

John raises both eyebrows. "What do you think?"

I accept the mirror and straw from John's hands, then snarf. Ouch. Shit. A fingerful of water in my nostril cools the burn.

I return the paraphernalia to John, who parrots my actions.

"Do you think I blew it?"

John takes his index finger from his nose and wipes a tear from his right eye. "Well, if you said those things about the baths to Gaby, I'd be r-e-e-eal pissed."

People are so touchy when it comes to their boyfriends.

My palms begin to sweat. I wipe them on my jeans. Blastoff.

"I don't see what the big deal is. You know Vic: I'm sick of covering for him. The lies. THIS BEHAVIOR MUST STOP!"

Through my righteous indignation I do feel tremendous guilt. I was coming down and therefore barely responsible for my mood swings. I have no intention of admitting this to John, who will get on the phone to Vic as soon as I turn my back. The politics of friendship.

John finishes his hair as he continues the conversation. "I think he's more pissed about the letter."

The letter. Handiwork of a martyr. I was justified. You are evil. Three pages.

"Well HE shouldn't have left that MESSAGE on my answering machine. The whole house heard it."

Before John can reply the bedroom door bangs open. A bottle of Drakkar falls off the shelf unit. GABY!

"YOU TOLD ME YOU DIDN'T HAVE ANY DRUGS, JOHN!"

Eyes are fiery with the rage of an addict scorned.

"He brought 'em." John points at me.

"Fuck you, John. I know you had them. I was outside your window. I heard everything."

Isn't Gaby just the type: crawling around on his hands and knees in a flower bed, spying. Like vermin. Just where does trust enter into ANY of my friends' relationships?

Here we go. I light a cigarette as Gaby launches his little tantrum. Most unattractive. I wonder how long this petit mal is going to last. Picking up the mirror, I cut a line with what patience I can summon.

"You're really fucked you know that John. Really fucked. I can't believe you. Holding out from me you little cunt. It's not fair. You're a fucking..."

Gaby stops screeching long enough to do the line I've offered him. Kids.

"Shit! I gotta get some water." Gaby retreats to the rest room.

I look anxiously at John. "I am *not* in the mood."

"Me neither."

It is a moment of perfect spontaneity. I grab the drugs. John grabs a jacket. Snickering, we run to my car. As the engine starts snickers give way to belly laughs.

In the rearview mirror, just before turning off John's street, I see the miniature silhouette of a disgruntled, frustrated boyfriend. He stamps comically.

Life is good.

TROY

I stand at a pay phone on Santa Monica Boulevard right outside the club.

"Hello?"

"Troy?"

"Hi!"

"Guess where I am?"

"Where?"

"Standing in front of Rage."

"I'll be right there, wait for me."

I hang up. My palms continue to sweat. I am so high. I feel like a whore standing here on this corner.

A man in shorts and a baseball cap walks by. A local on the prowl. He gives me the once-over. My nerves are shattered by the drugs. I actively avoid his gaze. The man laughs. "Get *her*," he says in an acidic tone. Get her...Miss Sketchy Thing.

I regret making the call to Troy. Wiping dampness from my brow, I realize the error. I don't want him to see me like this. Exit, stage left.

Too late.

A black BMW convertible pulls up to the curb, aborting my flight. It's Troy. Of course he drives this. We are, after all, in L.A. What else COULD you drive when you're young and successful in this town?

I get in the car. Troy leans over to kiss me. I knock the cellular phone off the cradle between us. "Sorry," I say, fumbling to replace it.

"It's OK," he says. "Calm down."

Troy's hand takes mine as we drive away. He's boyfriend material, all right.

I am informed that the townhouse is "a mess" and "custom-built" in the same sentence.

A mess? This? Not by my standards. Custom-built? And how. To the extreme. Circa 1984. The understated opulence of better times. Marble floors. Glass bricks. Berber carpeting. Crown molding. *Dynasty* revisited. Adam Carrington's bachelor pad.

Troy deposits me on an oversize white sofa.

"Would you like a drink?"

"Yes, please." Make it two. Hurry, goddamn it. My heart rocks my rib cage. Blood rushes through my eardrums.

Whoosh-whoosh-whoosh-whoosh.

I am high and intimidated. Intimidated by this man's physical beauty; intimidated by his success.

What do I have to offer him? I have the feeling that Troy is a control freak or worse. Maybe this is some kind of joke.

My host hands me a Bombay-and-tonic. Weak. Probably actually measured the gin with a shot glass. Accountants are meticulous, after all.

"You seem nervous."

"DO I?!" I laugh. A little manic giggle. The kind of twitter that would lead you to believe that something had misfired in the synapses.

After brief moments of conversation, Troy pounces on me. I spill part of the cocktail on white carpeting. "Don't worry about it," he says, sticking his tongue back in my mouth. An abrupt romantic style is sometimes favored by men in number-oriented careers.

I reach my hand up to caress the back of Troy's head. *What's this?* Netting? A WEFT! Horrified, Troy pulls away. I recognize the blatant fear of discovery in his eyes. I maintain a blank expression. Poker face.

HE'S BALD! That's the Achilles' heel. These golden locks are a chapeau of hair.

We resume kissing, this time less fervently.

My heart continues to pound, sweat pours off of me, I tremble. When foreplay becomes less playful, a flaccid dick betrays my little secret. The cursed crystal weenie. Dash it all.

"Are you on drugs?"

Well, what should I do? Tell him it's a war wound? Or better: It's your hairpiece.

I never get a chance to reply. Troy is decidedly anti-whatever I'm on. "I'd better take you back."

We drive a few tense moments back to Rage.

Wordlessly I step out of the car.

THE FIGHT

I walk past Rage's doorman as last call is announced. I order two gin-and-tonics. I suck down the first at the bar and saunter away clutching the second. Maybe I'll have time for a third. I wonder where John is?

The crowd has thinned out considerably. It is awfully late. Or is it awfully early? Is it just awful?

I am stunned by how quickly a romance can go awry. I can understand why. My impulsive self. If only I had suppressed the impetuous urge to call loverboy. BUT NO! Calling when I'm fucking tweaked out of my mind. Nothing like shooting one's self in the proverbial foot. Oh, well. He was too good for me anyway.

"Where have you been?"

I look into John's face. He seems anxious. So unlike him to worry when I disappear. "I went to Troy's house."

"Guess who's here?"

I look around the half-empty dance floor. Gaby.

"How'd HE get here?"

"Bart brought him. He's *mad*."

I don't wonder. Gaby has a volatile Latin temper. Although I have never experienced the wrath directly, I have witnessed him in action with John. I am not in the mood for any shenanigans tonight.

"Has he said anything to you?"

John shakes his head.

"He IS mad," I agree.

It's so unlike Gaby to let these things go. He did manage to seek us out. I wonder how many places in L.A. County he stopped before tracking us down. Probably started at the Sugar Shack in El Monte and headed west.

"How long has he been here?"

"Too long. About an hour."

"Should we cut our losses and escape now?"

"No way!"

I scowl at my chickenshit friend, who ignores me. I will not tolerate a public row.

"Shush! Here he comes."

If Gaby was merely angry earlier, he's absolutely enraged now. Stupid child. If only he knew how to behave. A few courses at Miss Crabtree's School of Grace and Etiquette wouldn't kill him. Charisma on Crystal; Poise Through Chemical Angst. I ready myself for the onslaught of vitriol by fixing a look of strident boredom on my face.

Gaby storms past us and exits through the club's front door without uttering a peep. Bart follows, shrugging his shoulders and smiling stupidly for our benefit. This is atypical Gaby behavior.

I turn to John, unable to conceal my shock. "Wow."

Surprise registers as silence. I perceive disappointment. I think John would have relished a fight.

The club's lights come up. All the way up. E-E-EEK! John, myself, and the other dregs of the early morning are driven onto

Santa Monica Boulevard.

Initially the fight is nothing more than a couple of tweaked-out queens shouting expletives at one another. It is at this time that I distance myself as lady-in-waiting to John, preferring to blend in with the gathering spectators. I am not about to acknowledge either one of them. Soon after they are shouting in each other's faces. When the first blow is drawn, the crowd and I gasp audibly. As the fight becomes maniacally vicious (complete with kicking and hair pulling, as if choreographed by the Women in Prison Dance Company), I push through the cheering mass and walk to my car. I'm over it.

I will languish in a bathhouse.

WHORE

take it, come on
and
fuck me
I don't care
it's free!
just take it, I'm easy
won't cost a cent
don't mean a thing
just take your time
take your fill
take what's left
of me
I don't care.
I'm a whore.
don't ask any questions
DO IT.
oh, yeah
oh, yeah
oh, yeah

oh yeah, before you go
let me ask you this:
did you fuck me
or
did I
Fuck You

COMING OUT

On graduation night Vic, John, and I—brandishing our adulthood like sabers and ready to experience Life—escape the dreariness of the suburbs for an evening of debauchery in The City. On the freeway in John's father's Granada, Vic announces that we are going to a club called The Odyssey. "It's 18 and over."

I have not yet turned 18, a fact I nervously point out to my cohorts. Vic turned 18 in the spring, and John, who graduated the previous year, is nearly 20.

"Don't worry about it. With your ass the doorman is bound to let you in."

"Will there be GAY PEOPLE at this place?"

Vic turns toward the back seat and lowers a "you've *got* to be kidding" look on me. Rolling his eyes with sophisticated grandeur, Vic resumes his face-front position in the passenger seat and pushes a B-52's tape into the stereo.

I look out of the window and think of the only fag I know, Byron Rhine. With long fingernails and breath of treacle, Byron is the school weirdo. I imagine a club packed with Byron clones.

What I discover in The Odyssey that night changes my life forever. Cute guys!

Tanned boys fuss, fawn, and flirt on the dance floor. I see boys openly making out on the patio. Punk boys with green hair make eyes at preppy boys with what will later become the fag coiffure ideal: highlighted wedge cuts.

It's Disneyland!

It should be. In the following weeks we quickly befriend some of the dancers from the Anaheim theme park who, like us, frequent the club's Wednesday and Friday "New Wave" nights. The hip people don't go on any other night. DJ Chuckie Starr plays disco the rest of the week.

We three boys from Medfly-quarantined West Covina cling dearly to the last vestiges of our supposed heterosexuality. Like hawks we observe each other's every move.

Who will be first to act out the horrible truth?

I sit with Vic and John at a small, round table, sipping mineral water and smoking clove cigarettes. When a techno cover of "Stupid Cupid" comes on, we dutifully take our places on the stage beneath the DJ booth and perform our choreographed routine to the beat. Everyone has a number except for Serenia Marie, who will dance for hours on a spotlighted podium to anything. L.A.'s dance queen later does a turn as the cover nymph for a series of *Rodney on the ROQ* albums.

Tony insinuates the lyric to Soft Cell's "Sex Dwarf." *ISN'T IT NICE...LURING DISCO DOLLIES TO A LIFE OF VICE...*

On a sweltering September day, as I imagine how Maggie the Cat would feel languishing in the miserable weather wearing a corset and satin slip, Vic phones with a fateful proposition. Roddy, the son of a pharmacist, has offered each of us a Quaalude if we slip a mickey to John, whom Roddy wants to bed.

"You know John's *gay*. I've seen him checking guys out."

"Me too!"

"This will just help things along."

I agree to help carry out the scheme.

RUN LITTLE DOGGY...LURE A DISCO DOLLY...

Vic and I drive out to Burbank to pick up three 'ludes from a very excited Roddy. Luckily for John, Roddy is cute. We agree to meet at "The O" at 11 that same evening, our drugged friend in tow.

We buy a bottle of reconstituted lemon juice at 7-11 and dump all but a few tablespoons of the liquid down the drain. John will supply the tequila to accompany the potent Spanish Fly Vic and I laughingly prepare. We can not resist making the obvious comparison to Lucy and Ethel as Vic crushes a round tablet, dumping the powder into the green bottle.

"We're poisoning Carolyn Appleby!"

We drink in the car on the way to West Hollywood. Vic drives so that John can shoot tequila in the passenger seat as we make the journey. I communicate with Vic in the rearview mirror. Raising eyebrows and spiked Big Gulp sodas, we silently toast congratulations as John downs the lemon juice. Our arrival at the boulevards Beverly and La Cienega is prompt. John stumbles as we approach the club's secured door. "Wow you guys, I'm fucked-up."

A triumphant glance from Vic. We pay the $8 cover and enter the club.

Roddy immediately accosts us. "How'd it go?"

We push our friend into Roddy's open arms.

John is forced from the closet. Vic and I willingly follow, free from our fear of each other.

Tonight we dance with abandon.

ORIENTATION

The employee parking lot. Another one. How many of these lots have I parked in? 20? 25?

I walk to the meeting room. Pulling on a blazer, I begin to feel professional. How is it that clothes can dictate my stride and attitude. If you look good, you feel good. Confident. By merely slipping on a tie and dress shoes, I have adopted a new outlook.

The Human Resources manager greets me at the door of the conference room. "Good MORning! How ARE you?"

Have mercy. It's only 8.

"Awake." OK, my outlook is not so new.

Undeterred by my curt answer, the manager continues on with his tirade of cheeriness. This man's every fiber is electrified with delight. A company guy. Those glazed orbs. I wonder if he ever had a lobotomy.

Breaking away, I approach a buffet table in the corner. A few sanitary cheerleader types mill about exchanging pleasantries. How white can we get? "Try the blueberry muffins," a culotted ingenue advises. "They're yummy." I do. They are. "I'm Candace, but everyone calls me Candy."

Well hush my mouth and shucky darn. Candy. How painfully appropriate. Bet she was popular in high school. I introduce myself as the new concierge.

"I'm a cocktail waitress!"

"With all that figure and enthusiasm, one never would have *dreamed*."

Candy beams. Poor vapid thing. When did life become so predictable?

I take a seat at a long conference table. Dum-dum sits next to me.

"I hope you don't mind! I just hate not knowing anyone, don't you?"

I nod. I would rather not tell the truth. That would require an explanation I'm sure, and I can just see myself drolly attempting to make Candy understand my ennui.

I take a drink of the vile coffee. What relation it has to Colombian beans, I do not know. Where is that Swedish bitch when you need her? "*Der coffee is bad? Try some of dis, and have dis cake too.*" If only life was like commercials—everything perfect in 60 seconds.

I smile at Candy and slide the cup and saucer away from me. I envy her, really. So lovely in a *Cosmo* sort of way. She's HAPPY. Doesn't know the difference. Life is like a Hallmark card. I would bet her greatest loss was Deborah Winger at the end of *Terms of Endearment*. How many people like this have I known? Too many. Products of television and sugar, as Mom would say.

Orientation begins with a getting-to-know-you game. Irritating. Vomitorious. Just plain stupid. *Quelle* Tupperware. We describe ourselves to the other group members and pair off. With crayons and marking pens, we are forced to draw little pictures of our partner's self-described personality. For Candy I depict a palm tree ("I LOVE the desert"), an ocean sunset ("I LOVE the beach"), a glamorous eye ("I LOVE makeup"), and a bull moose head ("I'm boy-crazy"). After all drawings are complete, we each share our handiwork with the group.

"What's the moose for?"

"She's horny."

Mr. Human Resources gags on a guffaw. Embarrassed, Candy covers her gaping mouth with her hand. I've won the getting-to-know-you game.

The rest of the grueling morning consists of one bore after another. A parade of gray-suited, gray-complected corporate management types welcomes us grayly. Each man is a caricature of the other, complete with the same bland haircut and nasal voice. All of the automatons tout an "open-door policy" and Employee Empowerment. A big, fat fucking deal is made of the latter although it is never explained. *Employee Empowerment?* Sounds like it was developed at the Church of Religious Science or by some crazed pop psychologist. Either way it doesn't mean any more dollars for myself, and so it is just a useless term meant to make me FEEL better.

I begin to stop hearing what is being said. It's amazing how life-like these men are. Like that scary Lincoln ride at Disneyland. All have been programmed at the same public-speaking seminar. The verbiage remains consistent, as do the hand movements. Arms bent at the waist, hands clasped in front, only to be extended to emphasize key words or phrases. This same body language is exhibited by politicians during those miserable campaign years. New Age ministers and motivational speakers are also guilty of this colorless gesticulating.

We are treated to each manager's history with Hyton Hotels. The stories vary little from one to the other. Devoted company people. That's how you get ahead. Devotion to the Company. The Company. Over and over. The same gestures, the same haircut, the same tailoring, the same vocal inflections, the same story, the same the same the same the same...

Candy elbows me in the ribs.

"Was I snoring?"

Candy nods sheepishly.

Gray men glower. I can only smile broadly.

Mr. Human Resources clears his throat. "On that note, let's break for lunch."

ORIENTATION

The second half of the day is facilitated by Mr. Human Resources' lovely assistant, Teesha. *Teesha.* Must have been named for the family's beloved Pekinese. She's obviously from the Midwest somewhere. "Pairk yer caire in the employee pairking lat." Those hard A's. What is it about that Kenosha accent? Some form of Wisconsin torture.

Teesha's well-rehearsed speech on sick days and vacations is choreographed with those hand movements. She's really gonna go someplace with the company. Yessir! Why is it that they have to emphasize with their hands, anyway? Is it to add drama? If so, these folks are obviously not trained in The Method. They are trained in Mediocrity. Does it require training, this need to be abjectly average? Teesha and the gang are obviously striving to be this way. Why?

After Teesha's performance the television takes over. Electronic training. Apparently, the videos were produced in conjunction with The Children's Television Workshop. We learn the ABCs of Quality Service. This is how to identify a drunk! This is how to throw him out! This is what *not* to do when a guest complains! This is the history of Hyton Hotels!

Old man Radzer bought the first Hyton Hotel near a California airport in 1953. He then built a worldwide empire. The name came from his majordomo, Hyton Fairfield III, who oversaw operations of the first hotel.

Small world.

I have had some subservient dealings with the wife of a Radzer son. Linda Radzer was a regular client of a tony salon on San Francisco's tony Maiden Lane. I was the tony receptionist in the tony mid-'80s. Tony clientele. My first exposure to absolute wealth. Spoiled brides of powerful business magnates and high-powered attorneys. One of a glamorous breed of Poor Little Rich Girls patronized this establishment on her frequent visits to the Bay Area. Preparations of vanity for Junior League balls and opening nights afforded me a glimpse into a lifestyle I had only imagined. Lovely gamines, hair and makeup in place, rushed off into the evening to dine, dance, and be seen in expensive gowns and jewels.

Linda Radzer was such a creature.

Linda and her best friend, Kara Lowenstein (the young show-girl wife of an ancient theatrical producer), would stand at the front desk and hash out ways to fill the day. The conversation went something like this:

LINDA: (*paying her substantial bill for highlights*) Kara, what do you wanna do?

KARA: I dunno, what do YOU wanna do?

LINDA: Let's do lunch!

KARA: I can't, I'm onna *DI-et*. Let's go shopping.

LINDA: I can't, I spent too much yesterday.

Each woman's delivery was most serious. A fellow receptionist and I would fight to keep from laughing aloud. Two nouveau riche princesses without a care in the world or an appointment in their Dayrunners.

During my final fling with heterosexuality, I dated the nanny of Linda's children. The biggest thrill of that relationship was rifling through the Villa Radzer refrigerator. Rich folks eat just like the rest of us. Diet 7-Up, Grey Poupon, cold cuts. Ketchup! The most exotic condiment in the door was a jar of capers. Big deal.

I return to my body when Teesha utters the word IN-surance. This is a crucial bit of information. I have been afraid to apply for insurance in the past, as disclosure of my diagnosis within the medical community could result in being blacklisted with the label PRE-EXISTING CONDITION. For patients with a terminal illness, the dilemma is whether to be truthful, and therefore be fucked by the establishment, or to lie and risk the chance of being sued or jailed or fined or all of the above. That rock and a hard place we all keep hearing about.

BUT WAIT, THERE'S MORE!

Say I go ahead and fill out this little form and disclose my HIV status. It has to be processed by the Human Resources office, and this information is quite delectable. Imagine the banter and speculation if word gets out. It's tough enough being openly gay, but I have no intention of being the token AIDS employee. I shall remain uninsured.

As the day comes to a blessed close, Georgeanne (call me Georgie) pokes her heavily made-up face in the conference room.

"Can I borrow Mr. Wonderful?"

Her phoniness is sickening.

I am excused. I collect the reams of scrap paper containing useless information and meet Georgie outside.

"How'd it go?"

"Great."

We walk toward the parking lot. Georgie slips an arm through mine. I don't relish this kind of familiarity with an employer, but she seems to have something urgent on her mind.

"Now I realize that this is your first week, and I may be going out on a limb by asking you to do this. It is above and beyond the call of duty as a concierge, but not as a Hyton employee. Do you follow?"

I nod.

"Well, your cooperation is not required, but it would be greatly appreciated. I know I can count on you."

Georgie smiles a big, cheesy grin and bats her clumpy, ever-flirtatious eyelashes. After the Buildup I am afraid to ask what is not being readily volunteered. I shrug.

"I guess you can count on me."

"Good," Georgie sighs. "Next Sunday, Easter, The Newport Resort sponsors an egg hunt for the children of our guests. What I need is someone who can oversee the hunt in a less-than-official manner. A special goodwill ambassador for the kids to relate to. Do you follow?"

Kids? Relate? Goodwill? I pretend to understand.

"I knew you'd be game. Why, I bet you'll be the best Easter Bunny we ever had."

SOME BAD NEWS

I sit in the sterile doctor's office, waiting.

A handsome blond man smiles down from a poster on the wall before me. So many teeth. Brilliant. Blinding.

You could never tell by looking at me, but I'm a person living with AIDS.

The heroes of HIV. A paid endorsement. *I did the hokey pokey and I turned myself around, death's what it's all about.* I don't buy it.

A basket filled with free condoms beckons. I shove a dozen into the pocket of my jeans. 12 fucks. Wishful thinking.

The monthly checkup. Funny. I almost look forward to them. All of the people I so liberally resented a year ago have come to represent comfort. Caring. Is this bonding? Stupid word.

The doctor knows me; I know her. She calls me by my first name. I recently spotted her playing pool in a dyke bar. High, I sank into the shadows and watched. You'd never take her for a doctor. Not without a lab coat. Just a regular person out with friends, laughing. Drinking.

The doctor is not in that humor today. The skin of her brow is taut. Serious. Fraught with…*concern?*

"There's a problem here." She flips open the chart, motioning to a computer readout imprinted with a string of numbers that are meaningless to me. "Your T-cells continue to plummet, the P24 antigen shows that there is viral activity, and your white blood cell count is so low that I couldn't put you on a retroviral even if I wanted to." The doctor tosses my file on the counter in disgust. "I don't know what to make of it."

She IS concerned.

"Oh, well, it's not your fault. Let's have a listen to those lungs."

I pull my shirt up around my shoulders, breathing as the doctor instructs.

I feel guilty. The doctor is more anxious about my health than I am. Perhaps now is the time to admit the truth.

"Well, the lungs sound good…"

"Doctor, I, I…" This is tough. "I have a question."

"Yes, what is it?" She hangs the stethoscope around her neck.

"That blood work. Could it be from my consumption of…of…ALCOHOL?"

She makes a note in my chart. "I won't say that it's not a factor, but this drastic change, well, I seriously doubt that it's the whole problem." She looks at me intently. "You know, you really should quit drinking."

"I know."

A long silence.

"Have you filled out one of these?" She holds up a Durable Power of Attorney for Health Care. I shake my head.

"Take this one with you. I'd like to have a completed copy of this form on file. Just a formality. Try and bring it in the next time I see you."

I walk to my car. I have completed that form. It lists Mom as the executor should I become incapacitated. That bitch. Now's the time to change it. But who? Who will take on the responsibility? I don't want HER pulling the plug.

It's the crystal.

It's killing me.

I don't care.

EASTER

Christ is risen! Christ on crystal? The shit would raise the dead. It sustains me; a walking cadaver.

Golden rays of morning peek over the horizon. John and I sit at the shore watching waves pound the sand. We partied all night; neither of us has slept. This extended silence is a welcome intermission from hours of banal conversation. The same talk we had last week and the week before. The same jokes and anecdotes. The same raised eyebrows. The same drug lore. Even the gossip is a rehash.

Fighting the ocean breeze, I light a cigarette. Maybe now is the time to approach a serious topic.

"John, I'm in a quandary."

My dull-witted friend turns to me. A big question mark hangs over his head. I have overstepped the boundaries of John's limited vocabulary. At least I have his attention.

"I…well, I saw the doctor this week. My monthly visit." This is harder than I anticipated. "My blood work looks, well, uh, funny."

"What's *funny?*" John does not look away from the monumental task of lighting another Camel.

"Just technical stuff. You know, numbers dropping, low cell counts."

"Oh."

Reaction: flat. I wonder if I'm reaching him? Doggedly I continue. "You see, uh, what I mean is, if something were to happen to me, something desperate…"

"You mean like you couldn't get a date again next New Year's?"

"Well, no, I meant something DIRE."

Blank stare.

"OK, say I lapse into a coma and I can't tell the doctors that I don't want to be on life support—are you following me?"

"I think so. You're unconscious, right?"

"Very good!"

HELEN: WA-WA.

ANNIE: (*Signing into Helen's palm*) WATER! GOOD! VERY GOOD!

"OK, I'm unconscious and I don't want to live, but I can't tell the doctor to pull the plug myself. I would want someone I trusted to see to it that my wishes were carried out."

"Like a pinch hitter?"

"Exactly." I've made the connection! I light another cigarette before continuing.

"With my blood work looking as it does, the doctor would like to have the proper form in my file in case something happens." I take a drag off the cigarette, pausing before getting to the point of the conversation.

"John, would you be my pinch hitter?"

Eyes widen. Lips pale.

"I don't know what I'd do."

"It would all be on paper. You'd just have to see to it that my wishes were carried out."

I look across the ocean, away from my distraught friend. The air is unusually warm. The sky is clear. Like summer. You can see the hump of Catalina Island adrift in the water 26 miles from the coast.

John flicks his cigarette onto the sand. "I don't want to talk about this."

Case closed. I concede.

My disappointment is profound.

HERE COMES PETER COTTON MOUTH

I drive directly from the beach to the Newport Resort. I finish off the last of the crystal in the employee parking lot before walking to the lobby. What the hell.

The Easter Bunny. Good Christ. It's as if this were some sort of initiation into a twisted fraternity. The Loyal Brotherhood of Hyton Employees. What wouldn't I give for a great big Bloody Mary.

At 8:30 A.M. the temperature is well into the 70s. It's going to be a scorcher.

I approach the concierge desk. Georgie rummages through the lower cabinets of a credenza. Bent at the waist, her knees straight, I have an unsurpassed view of the boxer-like control top of Georgie's panty hose beneath another minuscule skirt. Perhaps all of a yard-and-a-half of fabric went into the construction. Chick-yellow. For the holiday.

"Hi, Georgie."

She gasps. "God you scared me!" Georgie cocks her head sharply. "You look awful. Are you OK?"

I make the teeny-weeny sign with my thumb and index finger.

"I have a little hangover."

She shakes her head in disapproval. "Oh."

I am led to a large conference room adjacent to the hotel restaurant. Employees in HYTON CARES! T-shirts rush to create an ambience of fun for juvenile monsters. Hyton cares? Brother.

Balloons, crepe paper, cardboard bunnies. The whole undertaking has the feel of preparing for a junior-high sock hop. The employees go about their task with ferocious intensity. It's like being with the elected officials of the Associated Student Body. I'm sure this will be the most fabulous Easter since the Resurrection.

Georgie presents six flats of hard-boiled eggs to be dyed by me. Of course! What else does the Easter Bunny do? Fingers quivering, I go about my chore. Purple, green, blue, yellow. It takes about an hour.

I sit quietly watching the workers. They bug me. Silly company people. Enslaved for the paltry sum of $7 an hour. Very white middle-class. TV chatter abounds. That Matlock! Isn't he clever.

The time has come for me to don my costume. A big, fuzzy, white jumper. Feety pajamas. I look like a giant infant. Swell. Long, pink ears hover from the matching hood I wear on my head. I'll die of heat stroke. Oh, god...what's this? A ruffled organdy Elizabethan ruff. My humiliation is complete.

Make the most of it. Grace, poise, dignity. If anyone can pull this off, it's you. Using a borrowed eyeliner pencil, I draw a triangle nose and whiskers on my exposed face. Not exactly convincing. The metamorphosis will have to be in the delivery. How does one get in character when portraying a rabbit? I tuck my lower lip behind my front teeth. Oh, for that drink.

Reluctantly I step out of the rest room.

With some pomp and circumstance, moi, le grande lapin, am

escorted by the hotel general manager across vast acreage to the scene of the egg hunt. Valets laugh loudly as I walk through the entrance portico. Fuckers. How dare they laugh at me, the Easter Bunny! I haughtily raise my black nose and shake my cotton tail.

As we near the green, children begin to squeal and point glee-fully. "Hey, Easter Bunny!" they shout. I'm caught off guard by the adulation.

"Wave," the manager commands. I do. The kids are delighted. I AM THE EASTER BUNNY.

The children are adorable. (OK. I said it.) The offspring of wealthy WASPs. Tow-headed cherubs in linen. Boys à la Lord Fauntleroy, girls in Laura Ashley. Easter with the King Family.

Parents and grandparents stand off to the side, watching. They too are in their finery. Presbyterian matrons wearing fancy bon-nets just for the occasion. A few of them tilt their heads and utter "How sweet" and all that as they watch me with the kids.

Georgie walks over and whispers in my ear, "Go frolic on the lawn."

Frolic on the lawn? FROLIC? FROLIC! Fuck her. It's enough that I'm out here. I am not about to frolic! Frolicking went out with Marion Davies. Where'd Georgie even pick up that word?

I grab a basket of candy and, hand in paw, coax my diminutive friends out to hunt for treasure. A moment of my attention is as prized as these dyed eggs. I am shrouded in magic.

As it happens, the hotel has been the sight of Passover festivi-ties for the past two weeks. Yearly, a group called Pristine Passover takes over 200 rooms, a kitchen, and banquet facilities for cele-bration of the springtime Jewish holiday. Crossing the green, a family in traditional Orthodox garb finds itself in the midst of Christian hijinks. Jewish children, unaware of what Easter means, begin to seek out eggs and candy with their Christian counterparts. "What are *they* doing out here?" cry appalled white folks. A mother yells "*Get the prizes! Get the prizes!*" while following her little boys in yarmulkes. This scene in intolerant Orange County, of all places. WASP parents stand aghast as people who represent the persecution and death of "the savior" trod on a Gentile holy day.

Now I DO need a cocktail.

As the hunt comes to an end, I pose for pictures with adoring children. They love me. They BELIEVE in me. Swept away in effortless sorcery, I feel strangely like that Dr. Seuss character. My heart will not grow three sizes today (that is the stuff of fairy tales), but for a dazzling moment I will revere, and cherish, the marvel of innocence.

NEWPORT STATION

All dolled up, I drive my new car to a favorite Thursday night haunt, Newport Station.

New car!

New to me. 1986 Chrysler Le Baron Convertible. Burgundy. White top. Low mileage. The ultimate in ginch. The premier fag-mobile. I have suddenly added a few years to my age.

I slide an Ella Fitzgerald CD into the stereo. CDs in your car! I'm living the life. Ella croons the lyric of a Duke Ellington tune.

And when nobody is nigh…you cry.

That last line always gets me. I know this lady. Too well.

A couple of months at the Newport Resort has afforded me the opportunity to ride around town in piss-elegance. I was born for that job. Concierge. Hard to call it "work." Making people happy. Quashing complaints. Recommending shows, restaurants, and museums. Playing authority: critic. Low-end public relations. My nature. The tips are good, the commissions marvelous, and the guests love me. I am treated as peer rather than servant. Respected. I can even perform when under the influence. Now THAT'S a JOB!

Feeling saucy, I allow the valet to park my sedan. The pride of ownership. How wonderful to be bourgeois middle-class.

I have decided to appease my alcoholism and get tanked. What a word. Alcoholism. Almost clinical. It does describe all those generations of my family—although *dipsomania* has a better ring.

Compulsion. The family legacy. Handed down to li'l ol' me.

Ah, to live in a castle on the moors. Come! See the portrait gallery. Generations of my family immortalized on canvas. Please don't touch! Observe. The Wall of Blame. Note that each and every one of my ancestors holds a cocktail. Favorite libations. Here, flanked by his beloved hunting spaniels, is Sir Franchot of Tone, a martini clutched in his velvet-swathed hand. Next to him, in resplendent repose: his wife, the Princess Lucille LeSeuer. Magnificent! See how she holds a chalice as floating cherubs pour into it 100-proof Smirnoff, a gift from heaven.

"Double Bombay tonic." For a hefty fee the bartender obliges.

I turn and shuffle into the crowd. Newport Station. I've been coming here for over a decade. When I first obtained a fake ID, this place was known as "your disco destination." Thursday nights continue to retain appeal after all this time. Amazing. Look around the crowded room. How many of these people have I seen here over the years? A good many. Some are worse for the wear than others. All of us aging in the glare of flashing lights. Seems sad.

I push to the rear of the room and order a second drink from the other bar. A favorite fool-the-bartender trick. Cocktail Ping-Pong. Order from the front, order from the back. Drink twice as much without getting "shut off." Maybe I'm fooling 'em. Maybe I'm not. Who cares?

By drink three I'm halfway to realizing my goal. Cloaking myself in booze. The crowd has begun to look better through gin goggles. It works.

I'm being stared at. He caught me off guard. Shoulders back! Head up! I sneak a glimpse when he's not looking. Kinda cute. He'll do. I look around the room. Nothing else happening.

I set the empty glass on the bar and motion to the bartender. I look over my shoulder as he pours. Still looking. I smile. He smiles. I turn and pay for my drink.

Soused, I sidle up to the man and introduce myself. Brad is charming in an offbeat way. A former skater with the Ice Capades, he now teaches ice sports to kids in Santa Barbara, where he lives. Bet he has a cute butt.

An out-of-towner. Perfect. So easy to get attached for the duration of the visit, bid a touching farewell, and be rid of him. I will get a little fix of romance without the awkwardness of being truly involved. That fear-of-intimacy thing. A fling will satisfy my precious ego, prop my vanity, and give me a taste of Life. The fix I crave before going back to the chilling reality of an emotional retardation that disables. A disability cleverly disguised by the glossy veneer to which I tend fanatically. Such devotion to an outward appearance makes it easy to ignore the hollow fissures lurking beneath.

Empty? Shallow? Lonely? Perhaps. Intimacy is a danger. Exposure; devastation. The truth could be my undoing. A mask represents the person I want to be, not the person I am.

This grand deception is for me. Only for me. Fuck the rest of you.

"What's that? Las Vegas? You're going to Las Vegas. How wonderful! I LOVE Vegas!" I'm pandering for an invitation. I get one.

"I couldn't. I have to work."

"Call in sick."

I look at Brad. Why not?

"Well, I don't know. I haven't completed the probationary period."

"Who cares? Besides, you won't have to pay for the hotel. I've already taken care of it."

I like this guy. He speaks my language.

"Where are you staying?" I finish cocktail number four.

"The Mirage."

Free room. Nice hotel. Cute guy.

"You talked me into it!"

Brad smiles and offers me another drink. I send him off to the bar.

Opportunism. It's a wonderful thing.

VEGAS

I slip on a sleeveless denim shirt. WeHo, 90069. Rizzo masquerades as Jason Priestley, film at 11.

Georgie had a shit hemorrhage when I called to say that I had a "family emergency." Of course she did. That means she'll have to drag her fat ass into the hotel on the WEEKEND! Terror of terrors! Woe is she! It's disturbing to think that during peak-occupancy days—Friday through Sunday—the Newport Resort is void of any upper management. Assistants and "line employees" rule on those days that we could use real leadership. Not that the managers are real leaders, but it would be nice to have them backing us up as authority figures during the stressful hectic times. Corporate America and the Service Industry: a contradiction in terms. Perhaps that's why this hostelry has been awarded a measly two stars.

Las Vegas. It's been years since I've been there. I hope the cocktail waitresses at Caesar's still wear those tacky hairpieces.

Brad arrives at the appointed time. A punctual fag? A red-letter day.

On entering the house Brad leans close to kiss me. I turn my head and lips meant for mine land squarely on my cheek. You lose! A tad early in the day for romance. I'm inclined that way between 5 and 6. Cocktail time. It is then that the world and everyone in it takes on a special glow.

I'm going to need it.

Brad is nice. Just plain nice. Just plain. Nice. Not my favorite combination. Too easy. Perhaps I will feel differently later. The trip is free. Get over it.

"I brought a friend with me."

"Really?" I look away from the black nylon duffel bag I wrestle with. What does he mean by "FRIEND"? I hope I don't have to sleep with them both.

"He's someone I've known for a long time. His name's Randy. I hope you like him."

"I'm sure we'll get along just fine."

I snap the bag shut. I hope I like this Randy person, for everyone's sake. I doubt I will. I don't much care for Homo sapiens in general.

I follow Brad out to the rented Lincoln Town Car. Perfect auto for a road trip. His friend leans against the trunk.

"*Hi!*" Randy says, exuberantly. Mistake number one. Exuberance before noon.

I return the greeting as Brad introduces us.

Standing downwind of Randy, I am overwhelmed by a familiar scent. Hugo Boss? Ounces of it. Pe-e-e–yew!

Randy spies the bag slung rakishly over my shoulder. "Is that ALL you're bringing?"

I nod. One bag is plenty for three nights.

Brad unlocks the trunk. I see why the question. The compartment is filled with soft-sided brown luggage. Familiar yellow Ls and Vs emblazoned boldly on leather. FUSSY! I wonder if it's the real thing.

"Is that all YOU'RE bringing?" I query, grasping at humor.

I ride with my gift-with-purchase luggage in the backseat.

We barely hit the outer reaches of Orange County before Randy begins to irritate me. An "industry" person, Randy's endless conversation consists of name-dropping and "insider info."

"What DO you do?" I ask through tight jowls.

"I work at Video-tech Labs. Have you heard of them?"

I have not.

"We format films for videotape."

"I see." An insider. Give me a break.

Three days of this? How must he die? Gunshot? Drowning? Poison in his foo-foo juice atomizer?

"Do *you* work?" Randy asks in that West Hollywood lilt.

"Yes." I'm getting testy. Does it show?

"What line of work are you in?"

Should I answer with a salary figure or title? Thank God I left last year's W-2 form at home. "I'm in public relations."

My date turns from the passenger seat to stare at me. What? That's not what you told me last night! I wink. I'll let you in on the joke, nudge nudge.

Brad smiles slyly. At least he has a sense of humor.

P.R. That's all Randy needed to hear. I've been sized up and pigeonholed. As far as he's concerned, we're going to get along just fine.

As far as he's concerned.

VEGAS, PART 2: THIS TIME IT'S PERSONAL

We pull up to the door of the Mirage hotel after four or five hours trapped in a car without a moment's peace. One of those uncomfortable-with-silence types, Randy is. Every minute filled with diversionary banter. Randy's recent birthday party at The Ivy, famed Beverly Hills bistro, was the main topic of conversation. His fabulous gifts his fabulous friends not to mention his fabulous wardrobe purchased at fabulous stores accessorized with fabulous shoes and fabulous belts.

I'd love to smack him with a fabulous handbag.

Imagine. All of this fabulousness for a first-generation American citizen born to immigrants from one of those colonies floating in the Pacific Rim. And of all the fabulous towns in Southern California, they ended up settling frightfully close to Pomona. A fabulous place to move away from.

My ears ring from the intake of information. I am dazed and rather confused, when a bellman inspects the trunk.

"I'll get a cart," he sighs.

I follow Brad and Randy into the lobby. Holy Raging Tackiness, Batman! This place looks like a grandiose Tiki Room.

It would, perhaps, strike me as spectacular if I were from Missouri. However, I am from Orange County, the land that Disney built.

I hang back as the boys check in.

The bellman rounds the corner dragging a loaded cart. That pretentious luggage. Is Miss Joan Collins checking in? It wouldn't surprise me if Randy had a wig stand or two stashed in there.

The boys complete the check-in transaction. I follow the bell-cart from a distance, squeezing in the elevator just as the door closes.

The room is dinky. Not at all what I had envisioned—I mean, the Mirage...those rates!

Feeling very much the "kept" entity, I walk over to the window. Drawing back a sheer drape, I peer out at the pool, floors and floors below us. Pool View. Hmph. Brad creeps up behind me, cupping my chest in his hands. He whispers into my ear "Happy?" and kisses me on the nape of the neck.

"M-m-m-m-m. Anything to be away from work." I hate playing this role. *So delightfully, deliriously happy! You're the ONLY man for me.* They kiss. Fade out. The end. Bro-ther.

I offer Brad a cheek. Kiss this.

Wrenching free, I step away. I run a finger across the dresser top: the white-glove test. Clean. I open a drawer.

"Uh-uh-uh! That's *my* territory." Randy wags a finger at me.

"Sorry," I mutter. I have a finger for him too.

I sit on the edge of one of two double beds: the one away from the window. I'm sure Randy would like the view as well. Arms up, I stretch and fall back on top of a poly-fill bedspread. Three days. I'm here for three days.

Sigh.

Randy takes his unpacking ritual very seriously. A study in Anal Retention. Upon surveying the empty closet, he decides

that the hangers are inadequate and, calling Housekeeping, orders
more. "You need some too?" Randy asks, hand covering the
receiver. We don't. "Just send up about ten more. TEN! *Diez,
DIEZ!* Have you got an iron? Of *course* we need a board." Randy
rolls his eyes for our benefit. "Yes, yes. Right away. *Gracias*." He
slams down the phone. "Where do they find the help out here?"

Brad lies next to me on the bed. I close my eyes. Warm ice-
skater fingers fondle my torso. How many hands can one man
have?

"Do you want to see the tigers?" Brad asks.

"Yeah, go see the tigers," Randy says, not looking away from
whatever it is he's doing. "I need to take a disco nap, anyway."

I feel gloriously unwanted. We escape. In the elevator Brad
asks, "What do you think of Randy?"

I lose my eyebrows in my hairline.

"He's OK. He's just like that."

The door opens. Saved by the bell.

"Are they dead?" I ask, watching Siegfried and Roy's listless
white tigers through a wall of thick glass.

"Good question. I've never seen them move. Maybe they're
just tired from last night's show."

"Maybe they're marvels of modern taxidermy, like their dad-
dies. Let's get a drink." What I meant to say was "Let's get drunk."
Why worry Brad so early in the game?

I soon discover that worrying Brad is the last of my worries. He
eagerly matches me drink for drink. The hard stuff. No beer at
this end of the bar.

A few cocktails later:

"How do you know Randy?"

"We used to skate together. One of the shows here in town.
The Frigid Follies. That was a while ago."

The Frigid Follies. How gruesome. The chorus lines are bad enough in Vegas—think of them on metal blades careening around on ice. *Shecky Greene and Debbie Reynolds in* Frigid Follies! In the Arctic Lounge. Shows: 8 and 11. Admission included with dinner.

"We got to be good friends when we lived here. You can imagine why."

"Yes, I can imagine why. I can't imagine why you'd stay in contact."

Brad chuckles. "Well, I have a place to stay when I visit L.A. Maybe I'm an opportunist."

"Maybe you are."

Smiling, I order another drink.

90-DAY REVIEW

Georgie looks down at the Corporate Review Form as if the loopy Catholic schoolgirl scrawl did not belong to her. Disassociation from an unpleasant task: the review/reprimand.

"You've been with us three months now." Georgie's tone is most managerial. "This is the Hyton Review Form. As you can see you have been evaluated in a variety of areas in accordance with job performance. Some of it's good. Some of it's not-so-good. Let's start with the good stuff."

I've been evaluated so many times. It's all the same. No matter what corporation. No matter how low the salary. All this production to quibble over a miniscule raise that you're probably more than entitled to anyway.

I always achieve the same high scores in attitude and appearance. Being vain, my hair and bronzer sparkle like the shine on my teeth no matter what the day. It takes a bit longer than a fiscal quarter for the glimmer to wear off my attitude. Usually by month six I become belligerent and nasty, and by month seven I am avidly combing the classifieds, searching for another job for which I may start this whole process again.

"These are copies of Guest Comment Cards. See how many times your name is mentioned!" Georgie sounds like she's talking to someone who, not tall enough to reach the desk, is sitting on a phone book. "Aren't you happy? That's the most in the department."

WAS THERE A HYTON EMPLOYEE WHO MADE YOUR STAY A MORE PLEASURABLE EXPERIENCE?

My name. 13 times.

I smile.

"See, you are proud. Give us that smile again."

Good grief. I'm beginning to wonder if I'm going to get a raise at all.

"Now the weak areas."

Here goes.

"Attendance is a real problem for you, young man. Way, way, way too many sick days. And the tardiness. Tsk! Tsk!"

I look across the lobby, searching for a better explanation than what the truth implies.

"Also, there is a problem with overtime when you are here."

I look back at the living Gloria Head. "Georgie, I only stay late when I'm assisting a guest."

"Overtime is against company policy."

"I thought I was here to serve people, not a time clock."

I'm pushing it. Georgie's tone takes a stern turn.

"Sometimes we must say 'no.' You can't always give. We are not the Salvation Army. We have to maintain a profit margin. If you want to help people on your time, fine. You may NOT infringe on my budget. I will not compensate you for your goodwill."

"I thought we were a hotel."

Them's fightin' words. Georgie pulls out the stops.

"*OVERTIME IS AGAINST COMPANY POLICY. YOU ARE*

NOT AUTHORIZED TO STAY BEYOND THE TIME THAT
YOU ARE SCHEDULED. DO YOU UNDERSTAND?"

I nod.

"There have been some complaints."

"Complaints? From guests?"

"No. Your coworkers. They feel that you are out-performing
them."

"Out-performing! Do you realize how those two harpies talk to
guests? I'd be out-performing them if I told our VIPs to fuck off
and…"

"*LANGUAGE!*"

The front-desk staff begins to take notice. Lobby scenes are
unacceptable. Georgie lowers her voice, not the intensity.

"Listen," she spits, "there is no room for stars at that concierge
desk. Company policy states…"

"Company policy," I grumble.

"Company policy states that employee behavior *must* be uniform. Friendly, courteous, efficient. *No more.* You're just a little
(how should I say this) *flamboyant.*"

"FLAMBOYANT?!" I wave my comment cards. "Are these
flam-BOY-ant?"

"Look. I am not here to fight with you. I *am* about ready to
write you up for insubordination and send your ass—I mean—
hiney home for the day. Company standards are company standards. You have to live by the rules. Just tone it down."

I harden my glare. Georgie pleads.

"Who do you think picks up the slack when you call in? Me or
one of the 'harpies,' that's who. You can hardly blame them for
being resentful. It's great that you perform when you decide to be
here—just, please, decide to be here more often. And tone it
down." Georgie smiles. "Not everything has to be a production."

A guest in a bathing suit trots through the lobby on his way to the pool. He smiles and waves.

"Hey, thanks for the restaurant tip. The food was great."

I smile oh-so graciously, waving with benevolence. "My pleasure. Anytime."

Performance over, I turn back to Georgie.

"Do I get a raise?"

Georgie nods. "I've been authorized to increase your salary by 25 cents an hour. Congratulations."

How thrilling. I now make 7 dollars and 25 cents an hour. Ten fantastic dollars more per week. A movie. A Coke.

I suppose I should be grateful.

Dignity is cheaper.

BEAR

"I love-ded her, but she did me wrong."

Buddha-like, the woman is vulgar in her girth. Seated at the far end of an L-shaped sofa, Bear's ineloquence is poetic with anguish. John (whose big idea it was to come here after the bar closed) is edgy at the emotional turn of the conversation. He fidgets, restless, beside me.

In the alcove off the living room, a group of card-carrying lesbians play Hearts. I would bet that cards are not the only things these ladies are packing. Graduates of the Sybil Brand Institute of Charm and Imposed Sapphism, their conversation drifts naturally into the language of sailors. Actually the verbiage doesn't drift there. It is anchored in The Port of Neanderthal.

I had earlier in the evening proposed a toast to my hostess and her band of Marauding Mansonettes. Not because I was so high that I adored them. Hell, no! I'd have to be on glue. It was a matter of survival. I thought that, as the only WASPy fellow here, I might not make it home without the aid of an ambulance. Holding up a can of Keystone beer ($4.99 a 12-pack), I grandly announced:

"To the drug culture: a society which transcends the disparity of classes."

You can imagine how that went over. I have become a running joke, which is fine. Like, who wants to kill the man in big red shoes?

Bear looks into her spacious lap. "I met her in the House, Holmes. I love-ded her. She did me wrong. When I got out I wrote her every day. I promised her a place to stay when she got out. She wrote me too, Holmes. She said she love-ded me. She told me so."

Bear struggles for control. I feel sad for her.

"You should see the letters." A pause. A sigh. "She did me wrong."

Lost in the memory, Bear gazes away. On the edge of my seat, I am dying to ask her to proceed. A natural fear of persons nick-named for large hairy beasts overrules my instinctual curiosity. John looks to me with a raised eyebrow. Far too much emotion in this conversation for him. The primal screams of this clean-shaven William Conrad overwhelm my callow friend.

"After she got out of the House, Holmes, she come to live with me and my sister and my nephew. I promised her that. He's a good-looking guy, Holmes. Real good-looking."

So. I see. The picture takes a shape.

"He is my blood, Holmes. My blood. I had to forgive him. I had to. After I found them, *she* had to go. I have to forgive him. He is my blood." A pause. A sigh. "I wanted to kill her."

I will not ask if the ex-con's muse still walks the earth. She could be buried in the arbor, for all I know. I will ask Bear for her phone number before I go. She could come in handy for disposal of my future former boyfriends.

Bear looks at me, appreciating the interest in her plight.

"You're OK, Holmes."

"So are you, Bear."

In the bathroom I splash cold water on my oily face. It's human nature that transcends the disparity of classes. Life. Love. Infidelity. Bear's experience, though rife with prison sentences, is just another tale of despair. Like all of our stories. No different. It's learning. It's being alive.

I pat my face dry with a hand towel.

My return to the living room is met with a heavy silence. All eyes watch as I cross the room to resume my seat next to John. He alone does not gawk at me.

Knowing John as I do, I realize that my momentary absence has been crammed with information, all of it mine. The dirty laundry. I wonder what gems have fallen from John's forked tongue.

An eternity passes before Bear intrudes on the silence. "Your friend says you're dying, Holmes."

The most precious gem. A diamond. I look at my "friend," silently demanding an explanation. He avoids my glare. I know why he did it. Anything to stay on top. I've simply commanded too much of the hostesses' attention. I loathe John's desperate pettiness. He is not the friend I went to high school with.

Can we stoop any lower? Have we lost all honor?

Was it ever there?

NEWPORT STATION

A Santa Ana wind blows stars through a balmy sky. A night for flawless romance. A lousy night for an arrest.

Handcuffs cut painfully into my wrists. Best not to struggle with them. They tighten up when I do.

"I'm cold."

I look over at John, who leans shoulder to shoulder beside me against the trunk of my car. How ill he makes me. It's 75 fucking degrees. I'm cold indeed. Wait until he spends a night in the hoosegow. Ah! To sleep in the same room you pee in. Charming. I understand the breakfast bologna is delightful.

I'm going to jail.

It was inevitable. Naturally, being prone to productions of epic scale, I've been cuffed in style. Standing in the crowded parking lot of Newport Station, I am embarrassed beyond compare. A white-hot glow of illumination comes from the headlights of a security vehicle. A gathering crowd of revelers enjoys the spectacle: silhouettes behind the glare of a V-8 spotlight.

Puffed up with pride, the security guard jots down the license number from the front plate as we wait for the police to arrive.

His big bust for the day. Some real excitement in his lamentable existence.

"The car's history."

I clench my teeth. My new car, property of the police. I'll be making payments on it long after it reaches the auction block.

My life. My luck. Shit.

We were only DOING drugs—not selling them. I wasn't driving. Is this reason enough to handcuff me? The shit wasn't even mine.

The police arrive with the expected display of pomposity. Lights flash. Sirens blare. The spectators buzz with interest: *What's going on? Who are they? Were they sucking dick? DRUGS!*

John looks at the ground. Jaw thrust out, I maintain a regal stance. This is my moment! Could someone touch up my face powder? I'm shiny and indisposed. Max, I'm ready for my close-up! What will Liz Smith say in her column tomorrow?

Officers faux and real confer about the situation. The little bald man is really quite delighted. He's having a very jolly Dennis Franz time of it. Self-satisfied, he tucks his thumbs into the belt loops of his permanently pressed trousers. A flaccid midsection jiggles with the intake of each breath as he excitedly apprises the police officer of the gory details.

The officer motions to John.

"You're on," I whisper.

"Does he want to talk to me?"

The officer answers, "Come over here."

John walks away out of earshot. Tall and tan, Officer Babe grills my co-bustee. The hunk stands with his back to me. Great ass! My only blessing in being incarcerated. Got to look at the bright side. The officer turns and looks over his shoulder as John pleads his case. I can only imagine what is being revealed.

John walks back to the car and, as usual, avoids my gaze. "He wants to talk to you."

I walk over to Officer Babe.

"Your friend tells me that the stuff belongs to you."

So. That's the game. I'm supposed to lose my car and take the rap. Fucking goddamned son of a bitch John.

"He's lying, sir."

"Did you pay him for drugs?"

I shake my head violently. "No, he offered them."

"So the drugs are his?"

"Yessir."

The officer turns to the security guard. "Where did you find the evidence?"

"Between the passenger seat and the door."

"Where in the car was this man when you apprehended them?"

"The driver's seat."

Squinting, the officer examines me for a moment.

"I said the drugs are his, sir."

The officer turns back to the security guard. "Release him."

The security guard removes the cuffs from my wrists.

"We're going to let you go," the officer says sternly. "I suggest you go directly home."

"What about my car?"

"Drive carefully. Don't let me catch you on the streets again."

Freedom! I walk past John and open the car door. I swallow before growling.

"Get off my car."

I drive past a string of onlookers onto the street. Once safely out of sight, I pull over and put the top down. Gusty winds whip through my hair.

Flawless night for an arrest.

THE LIVING END

Carbon monoxide has a strange odor. Not what I had expected. More chemical than smoke.

I lay back against the headrest. How long will it take? Will it be painful? Coughing? Vomit? I listen to the quiet hum of the engine and breathe…breathe…breathe…

Good GOD! I'm DEPRESSED!

Gagging, I punch the button on the garage door opener remote. I back out of the driveway and onto the street. Breathe. Fresh air. I drive a few blocks to the beach, parking on the street.

"Well, you almost did yourself in that time, you idiot," I exclaim to the breeze.

And for what? For what? For fear of cleaning up a little? For disappointment in a friend of so many years? For the realization that life's beyond control? FOR THE ABSOLUTE DRAMA? What drama? It would have been a most predictable outcome for a most predictable character. Self-destruction is not new, you know. It's not like you pioneered it.

Quelle dull.

Going the way of Dan White sans Twinkies. Thelma Todd sans

bruises. Ridiculous! As if more than four people would have mourned *mon tragique* passing. Intimate gathering of loved ones: "It was his destiny," they'd say. "I foresaw this years ago."

You fool.

I step out of the car and walk to the edge of the sand. I'm barefoot. Unshaved. Wearing a robe. Ah, the tragedy! Ah, the waste! Ah, the death of a bum!

I hate my life. I'm bored with the drugs. The high is just a high. It is artificial. I'm sick to death of my family and friends waiting for me to die. I'm tired of waiting to die. Of killing myself gratuitously.

"I AM NOT DYING! DO YOU HEAR ME? I AM NOT GOING ANYPLACE!"

Yelling to the ocean. Hear me, fishes! Hear me, crustaceans! Hear me, Neptune! I am not dying! *I'M BORED!*

I am a bore. A burdensome, bothersome bore. Predictable. A victim. Boring.

I AM NOT A VICTIM!

I thrust my hands into the terry cloth pockets at my thighs. What now? What to do? I can't die a waste. I don't want to die wasted. I'm young. I'm smart. I'm a good concierge.

Time to move. Gotta get out. Gotta run.

Run!

This time I'm not running away from Life. I'm running to it.

LOS ANGELES

I've never seen the president of a premium cable network behave in such a puerile manner.

"I get my car from the same rental agency every time I stay here, they should KNOW the phone has to be INSTALLED in the car." He throws the vinyl case containing a portable cellular on my desk. "This is ABSURD!"

Through the machine-gun staccato of verbiage, I've managed only "yessir," "I understandsir," and "I'm sorrysir" intermittently. The harsh accent native to the other coast is as repellent as the decibel range Mr. Big Shot insistently speaks in.

He continues to shout as I phone Luxury Car Rental, urging them to please rectify this emergency posthaste. "They'll be right here, sir."

The phone rings. I ignore it momentarily.

"They'd better be or I'm really going to raise some hell."

I smile until Mr. Big rounds the corner, out of sight. "Good afternoon, concierge desk."

"Good ahftah-noon. This is Lady Orwell's personal assistant, and I was wondering if you would be so kind as to make a reservation for four at 8:30 at Spago, please?" The accent hails from another continent. The voice is silken and polite.

"It would be my pleasure."

"Thank you. I do appreciate it evah-so-much. Good-bye."

The English. Such impeccable manners. So lovely. All that "please" and "thank-you" and "charmed-I'm-sure." But as liberal as they are with social niceties, they are equally stingy over crossing the proverbial palm with a Buck.

I ring Spago. "I'm calling from the Brentwood Duquessa. I need to make reservations for four at 8:30."

"Can't do it," the voice says, flatly. We could take them next Thursday before 6:30."

"It's for Lady Orwell," I counter.

"THE Lady Orwell?"

Correct.

"Orwell. Four. Eight-thirty. We'll see them then."

Hollywood's idea of clout. A Grande Dame of the thea-tah, Lady Orwell recently lost that big Award Motion Picture Actresses Seek to a younger, less-able technician. The nomination made a household name of the British Subject, which is handy for securing reservations in restaurants where the business of Nobodies is unappreciated.

The desk is littered with scraps of paper on which I've jotted endless notes pertaining to the demands of a very demanding clientele. I need to tie up loose ends before clocking out. Sinking into the padded chair, I take advantage of momentary peace.

Nestled in the hills above L.A., The Brentwood Duquessa caters to quite a different clientele than did the Newport Resort. No longer do I haggle with guests over rental car prices and recommend eateries based on budgets. It's top dollar all the way! although the hotel itself has fallen scandalously into disrepair.

Many of our more discerning guests have taken their business to The Peninsula, Luxury Hotel of the Moment.

Spencer walks from his post at the front desk. "What was all the calamity?"

"Wrong kind of phone in the car."

"I see."

Educated at the nation's finer institutions, Spencer boasts a last name that is closely linked to an American dynasty. His top-drawer drawl is way Buckley-esque. Attempting to "be his own person," my WASP colleague is a fugitive from familial responsibility, masquerading as a desk clerk in this hotel.

"Dahlia and I are going out tonight. You're coming with?"

"Dinner's on me," I reply.

The phone rings. Shit. I roll my eyes and wearily reach for the receiver.

"What's the word on my fucking cellular?!"

I stick the eraser end of a pencil up my nostril until it dangles freely and very calmly and professionally update Mr. Big on the situation.

Spencer returns to his post.

HOME

Two messages. I listen as I remove the tie from my neck. BEEP! *"Bueno? Jorge? Jorge?"* CLICK. Wrong number. BEEP! "Hi, it's Dahlia. Give me a call when you get in. I want to ask you something about Spencer. Bye."

I strip, don a dressing gown, and walk to the bar to fix myself a drink before returning the call.

I've taken an apartment in a slum known as Koreatown, not for the exotic cuisine, but for the wealth of architecture from the 1920s. This side of the tracks is more affordable than the Westside. While the businesses are mostly Korean, and Korean dollars bought up surrounding apartment buildings, most Asian slumlords live wisely outside of the immediate area. My neighbors are largely El Salvadoran. They are far less nosy than the lily-white aborigines that inhabit the shores of Huntington Beach. This neighborhood-unwatched community gives me a thrilling sense of anonymity.

The apartment building was erected in the midst of L.A.'s Deco period. Elaborate Crown molding graces 12-foot ceilings. Period chandeliers hang in the dining and bed rooms. Ceramic tiles of lilac and black line bathroom walls beyond a magnificent dressing chamber. I have chosen to furnish the immense living room in secondhand Cocktail Moderne. No set designer could have lit the room more dramatically. The overall effect has allowed me to live in the shabby glamour that I love. Fantasy and reality are merged. Life is bliss.

Swizzle stick clinking, I call Dahlia. "You want to talk about Spencer?"

"What do you think of him as a boyfriend?"

"For me or for you?"

Dahlia laughs and exclaims: "For ME, of course!"

"Dahlia, you're joking!"

"Why do you say that?"

"Good christ, my dear, Spencer is as gay as organdy in Maytime. Has he kissed you?"

"Well, kind of formally goodnight."

"I rest my case." A swallow of my drink.

"Are you having a cocktail?"

"Of course. It is happy hour, after all. I suggest you have one too."

"I'll wait till we get to Cava. So you don't think Spencer and I..."

"Do please stop with this. Unless you want a lot of heartache, I suggest you cool it with Mr. Blueblood."

"But he's so cute."

"Adorable. You do know how to pick them, Dahlia. If I'm not mistaken, your last boyfriend hung himself."

"I hate when you joke about that."

I hear Dahlia's agitation over that last remark. I have stepped over the line.

"Sorry, doll. I couldn't resist. Are we still meeting at 8 o'clock?"

"Yes. 8 o'clock."

"See you then?"

"Yes, you bastard. See you then."

ON THE TOWN

The actor/waiter presents me with the dinner check and a pen. I grandly autograph the bill and push the vinyl folder to the end of the table.

"How much should we tip?" Spencer asks.

"Twenty will do."

Dahlia and Spencer insist on supplying the tip. I've supplied the meal. Rather, the meal's been supplied to me.

An enviable benefit of being a concierge is the way restaurants court one's business. I regularly receive invitations to dine gratis at the finest Los Angeles bistros in exchange for recommendations to my guests. A subtle form of bribery. It works.

"Let's stop for a nightcap."

Behind the wheel I think of my two friends. They seemed cozy enough over tapas, yet I can't quite get past Spencer's foppish behavior. Camp all the way. The googly eyes did seem sincere, but a masquerade can be executed with the sincerest of convictions.

What do I care?

To each his own. I've warned her. She'll have no one to blame but herself. Hell, eventually they could guest on *Ricki Lake*. "My

Boyfriend Sells Antiques, today at 2 on RICKI.*"*

I care about my friend.

Imagine. A dangling corpse. In the garage. Your lover. You had

    no idea

            that

                things were

                    that

                        bad.

Only recently has Dahlia recovered from the shock.

I rejoin my friends at Atlas Bar. They stand passively holding hands.

The Society Orchestra plays music of the Jazz Age. Youthful clubgoers do period dances to period tunes. Where do these kids learn to do the Lindy and the Charleston?

Through a booze buzz I've been transported. Am I in West Egg? Will Zelda disrobe again? I would swear this gin was manufactured in a bathtub.

Dahlia interrupts my fantasy. "Isn't that Stew Stewart?" She motions toward a linened table.

"My god, darling, it is! And he's with his titled wife."

A bimbo by birth, the publishing magnate's spouse purchased her nobility from a Beverly Hills pretender to a throne. The Prince's marriage to a certain former Czech beauty queen gained him a gaggle of small dogs and a breathing scandal factory. Her recent tussle with a salesgirl in an exclusive department store over stolen merchandise earned the Princess plenty of publicity and a brief jail sentence to boot. Together they rule over an undisclosed European principality. I assume it's Moldavia, where, you'll remember, a tragic terrorist act killed Steven Carrington's male lover and forced Alexis to be foisted across enemy lines in a nun's habit. Now, the Pope may denounce birth control as a sacrilege, but if you ask me, the very idea of putting Joan Collins in holy garb should warrant a Vatican protest equally as vehement as the march against condoms. Far be it from me to question the judgment of a man in moiré.

Down the bar on the left is a group of guys obviously noticing Spencer and me. Spencer notices them too, though he quickly notices Dahlia when I notice him noticing them.

It doesn't take long for the trio to walk over and introduce themselves.

I introduce myself and then my friends, adding "He's straight." Best to annihilate the competition early on.

Smiling as if the canapés Julia Child just served were really quite wretched, Spencer turns away, drawing Dahlia into him.

I chat with the three briefly before deciding to leave with my friends.

Dahlia and I wait for Spencer to come out of the rest room.

"What did you guys talk about?"

"Spencer."

"And the consensus?"

"Puh-le-e-eze! He's a fag."

Spencer walks up. "What are you two laughing about?"

"Those characters I was talking to."

"They seemed kind of fey to me," Spencer sniffs.

I look at Dahlia slyly. I'll let that one go.

APOLOGIA

"COVER PHOTO BY VIC MASTERSON."

I turn from the credit on page three back to the cover. It's good. The photo's good.

Hmph.

Vic's work regularly graces the cover of this publication. He's built himself quite a reputation for shooting beefcake stills. Low-end Herb Ritts.

My initial reaction is jealousy, as it always is when the topic of Vic comes up. For 15 years I have harbored bitter resentment at Vic's hard-earned successes in career and love. Here again, Fatso scores.

That envy thing. It has, frankly, been the constant bone of contention in an otherwise smashing friendship. This animosity has worked both ways, although Vic is more genuine in his happiness for friends. My goodwill is laced with bile.

I stare at the half-naked torso. It's a beautiful shot. Vic has cultivated an artistic talent.

Vic's natural ability has traditionally been people skills. The gift of persuasion. An eye for raw talent. The vision to shape the talents of others into something magic. Hocus-pocus that led to early success in managing Amazonian freaks of beauty. Models.

He believed in me. Since high school. Through our fashion design failure. That debacle came after quite a buildup. The loss of money was more interesting to the local paper than our earlier press releases. It was my name printed on those labels. For me the early devastation meant defeat. For Vic it was simply another of Life's lessons. He gamely lumbered into new situations and triumphs while I staggered into darkened cocktail lounges and fell out of men's beds. A good photographer. A good friend. I miss him.

I've never been good at admitting when I am wrong any more than I'm adept at apologizing. Perhaps now is a good time to start?

I call the number listed on the magazine's credit page. Posing as a model, I obtain Vic's new number from the art department.

Anxiously I dial, wary of what Vic might say to me.

One ring.

Two rings.

Three…

"Hello, Vic? HI! Please don't hang up. I have something I want to say."

KATHERINE

A cellular phone rings. No fewer than six "industry" types scramble for bags or jacket pockets slung over chair backs. A suspendered fellow triumphantly barks orders into the offending portable device. Annoyed with the interruption, other quasi-moguls resume conversations in urgent tones better suited to Pentagon officials in wartime. Loudly discourse moves from the wonders of *Baywatch*'s stunning worldwide syndication success to the boffo box-office receipts of Jean-Claude Van Damme's latest plunder of the dramatic arts.

Where the hell is Katherine? That woman is always late.

"More coffee, sir?" I smile at the busboy and push my cup toward him. Housed in an ancient film studio, this restaurant boasts great coffee, exquisite scones, and the kind of themey ambience that attracts a very L.A. clientele. It's also Katherine's favorite breakfast spot.

"Well, you're here!"

"I'm HERE!" Smiling, my co-concierge sets a plate and coffee service on the table as she sits. "Did you read Liz Smith today?" She motions to the Calendar section in my hand. I turn back to page two. "Petra Katsand's playing Vegas. Her first concert in years!"

I groan.

"You don't like her?"

"La diva Katsand? The bargain-basement Callas? I think not!"

"That's right. You hated *Ocean King*." Katherine bites the end of a ginger scone.

"A grandiose slug of a TV movie in which the heroine acted with the aid of heavy filters and amber key lighting," I hiss. "And the stink she raised for not being nominated! Now Vegas. You can imagine what they'll charge for tickets. At least she's finally where she belongs—down the street from Don Rickles."

"Well, I like her. Nicholas will be thrilled!"

I cringe. "You're batting a thousand today, Katie."

"You two," Katherine sighs. "I don't see why you dislike each other so. You really are similar in so many ways."

"Eurotrash," I say, dismissing the subject.

"EUROtrash! That's awful," Katherine goads.

"Well, really. That watered-down b-r-r-rogue could only be the raison d'etre in Los Angeles. In the British Isles he'd be nothing more than a guttersnipe—the son of coal miners."

Katherine removes the cup from her lips, replacing it in the saucer. "You two bicker like a couple of old ladies. I'd say you were jealous of each other."

I cross my arms and grunt.

"I hope you won't be angry with me."

"Why would I be?"

"I invited him to join us."

So she did. No sooner than the words fall from her lips does Nicholas appear. And we're wearing the same shirt!

"Kather-r-rine," Nicholas coos. "I didn't realize there would be thr-r-ree."

"Nor did I," I sneer.

Katie shoots a "be nice" glance.

"Did you hear about Petr-r-ra Katsand?" Nicholas asks.

"We were just talking about her," says Katherine.

"AND about you," I say. "Were your ears ringing?"

"R-r-resoundingly," Nicholas says icily.

"Rip-ping," says I, veddy uppercrusty.

"Nice shirt," Katherine says. "You two look like twins."

Without comment Nicholas turns and walks to the bakery to order a scone. Katherine gazes after him. "He looks good today. I think he just had his hair done."

"Bleach."

"Said the kettle to the pot."

"Mine's tint! I'm gonna kill you, Katie."

"Don't get in such a huff. I have a hunch that you two will be friends in no time."

"No time's not breakfasttime. Certainly no time before noon. Don't forget, I have to work with him tonight. Manager On Duty. Big deal."

"So it's not his hair color. It's his position. Admit it, you're jealous."

"Am not."

"Are too."

"What is this, anyway? Dueling Dandies?"

"I think you two should be friends, that's all. Hush now. Here he comes."

"And here I go."

"*Don't!*"

"Leaving alr-r-ready?"

"Retreating."

"You mean r-r-retiring?"

"I meant repair."

"R-r-resuscitate?"

"Regurgitate."

"R-r-revolting."

"Ra-ther."

"R-r-rascal!"

"Rapscallion!"

Black pupils ringed with gold. 14-karat flecks dot the iris. I'd never noticed.

Nicholas.

I turn and run.

PRESTON

"We've got to go get Preston."

I change ears and yawn into the phone. "Where is he?"

"West Hollywood jail. You're the only person with a car I can get hold of."

"What time is it?"

"5:30." Vic's agitated. "Look, are you coming or not?"

"Do I have a choice?"

"NO."

"I'm on my way." I hang up and sleepily search for sweats.

Emerging from the West Hollywood precinct, Preston looks no worse for the wear than if he'd spent a night at La Costa. I soon realize that the pep in his step comes from a lovely pair of suede loafers.

"They're Gucci!" Preston exclaims as he climbs into the back seat. Vic looks over the frame of his glasses at me.

"Who'd you roll for those, doll?"

"A gift from Mater. Speaking of rolling, has someone got a light?"

"Preston! How did you get that past the police?"

"Well, they didn't STRIP-search me, dear."

I toss Preston a lighter and start the car. Before we're out of the station parking lot, I am handed a lit joint. I won't even think of where it's been.

"What an ordeal! I need a drink."

"Preston! It's 6:15 in the morning." Vic's the puritan of the group. I'm with Preston.

We end up nestled on bar stools in a very busy drinking establishment on Hollywood Boulevard. Our clique is the most animated of the crusty patronage.

Sipping martinis, Vic and I sit transfixed as Preston spins a yarn. (I will translate.)

"It all started as I was leaving a smart dinner party (supper of cocktail garnishes) given by my dear friend, young Lord Twombley (Eurotrash I hardly know). After a few (seven) imbibements, I was merely tipsy (tanked) and very tired because I had been out late on a date with the CUTEST guy the night before (I was doing crystal with a trick and haven't slept since Tuesday). As I motored (drove) down SanMo (Santa Monica Boulevard), I saw the flashing lights behind me. 'Bloody hell!' ("Shit!") I exclaimed, and pulled off to the side of the road."

"Were you very drunk?" I ask.

"No more than usual (in blackout mode), but I did have a cocktail in my hand, which I promptly poured on the floor."

"Pres-ton," Vic groans.

"The first thing the officer said to me was *'Why on earth are there ice cubes on the floorboard?'* at which time I handed him the glass and got out of the car."

"There-yago," growls a voice from behind. We turn to find the entire room enthralled with the story. Preston continues, playing to an impromptu audience.

"Well, the police couldn't have been lovelier, really. Considering the situation, they were just grand. You know, I must say that the coffee left something to be desired, particularly when compared to the café served in that darling bastille in the South of France."

Preston has been incarcerated on several continents. He is a learned scholar of prison cuisine.

"Of course, I couldn't have phoned La Dragonessa (mother), so I phoned Vic instead. Butterfly kisses to you both." Pinky extended, Preston downs the last of his martini. "The WORST thing is that I will have to go to those *dreadful* AA meetings. My WORD! I shall have to be quite drunk in order to endure those PEO-ple."

This utterance brings a rousing cheer from an audience of drunkards.

Preston pops an olive into his mouth. "I'm famished. Shall we go?"

Sweeping toward the door, Preston executes a Dior turn, genuflects, and blesses the crotchety multitude with "Salud, my friends, and…bottoms up!" before strolling into the street.

FRIDAY

"Your brothers!" The voice on the phone is exasperated.

"They ruined Thanksgiving. RUINED it. You're lucky you had to work, that's all I can say."

A family showdown. I hate holidays.

"What'd they do, Mom?"

"They got into a fistfight, those little bastards. Can you believe it? A FISTfight. In front of the house!"

Dahlia walks into the communication office to use the fax machine. I shift aside so she can access it.

"Mom, it's been coming for a long time. Those two have always hated each other." I hold the phone away from my ear and stick my tongue out at Dahlia.

"But they're brothers," says the voice on the other end. "How could they do this to me? On a holiday! I could kill them."

"You should have done that years ago. Do you ever listen to me?"

"Well, it won't happen again—that much I *can* tell you. I'm canceling Christmas."

"WHAT!"

"You heard me."

"Have you let the Macy's people know?" I ask drolly. "It is the busiest season for retail."

"Don't be a wiseass. I will no longer host your brothers' free-for-alls."

"I suppose this edict includes Easter as well."

"All holidays inclusive."

The Perry Mason tinge unnerves me. "Mom, I gotta go. I'll talk to you later."

Dahlia removes a stack of papers from the receiving tray of the fax machine and hands them to me for distribution. "What was that all about?"

"Just my mom canceling Christmas."

"Sounds harsh."

"That's my mom." On to other topics. "How was your holiday?"

"It was fun. I went over to Skip's house and partied with his friends."

"Who the hell is Skip? Last I heard, you were going out with that Jimmy guy."

Dahlia laughs. "I am."

I look down my nose mockingly. "Ah. I get it. So you're done with Spencer?"

"Through. A girl's gotta get it sometimes. There was NOTH-ING going on with Spencer. I was lucky to get a peck on the cheek."

"He's a fag, I'm telling you." Now the dirt. "Are you sleeping with both those guys?"

"Well, why not? I'm sick of the double standard. It's OK for you guys to sleep around, but if I do it, I'm a slut liable to be stoned in the streets. Give me a break. I'm wearing a damn A on my chest and I'm not ashamed. Besides," she adds primly, "I don't really want a commitment right now."

"Why is that?"

"I just don't want one now, OK? Gawd, what's with all the questions? I feel like I'm back home in Kansas City."

Katherine walks into the office. "There you are! We need you out front. A guest is asking for you."

"I'll be right there." I pass the faxes to Katherine and turn back to Dahlia. "Please don't be angry with me, doll. I have no judgment of you. I'm just nosy, ya know? Not to mention all that SEX. I'm chartreuse with envy!"

Dahlia smiles. "No biggie. Maybe now you'll let me be one of the boys?"

"I dub thee Sir Dahlia of the queers."

PAGAN

"I'm a paid whore."

I look at my upstairs neighbor. Raising the martini to my lips, I stall a reaction. I'm sophisticated after all. Really.

"And you waited this long to tell me?"

"I had to make sure you could handle it. You *can* handle it, can't you?"

"Of course." I look out of the window over L.A. rooftops at the monstrous downtown skyline. It's beautiful at night. An emerald city sparkling in a dust bowl.

This explains everything. The pager. The odd hours. The two or three names he goes by. I recently christened him with another, Pagan, for the low altar he has in his living room. I look at the photos of deceased family and friends. A cat. The memories he religiously keeps alive.

"How much do you charge?"

"Depends. $75 in. $100 out."

"An hour?"

"An hour."

My goodness. That's a good living. Four tricks a week would

cover my expenses and then some.

"Are you busy?"

Pagan sets his glass on the coffee table, shrewdly examining my curiosity. "I can't complain. The advertisements help. I'm glad I don't see too many new clients anymore. That can be scary." He motions to a solitary olive framed by an arid glass. "Are you ready for another?"

I nod.

Pagan takes my glass into the kitchen. He pours gin and vermouth into a mayonnaise jar half filled with ice. After screwing the lid on, he proceeds to shake violently, thereby beating the hell out of what was a fine liquor from a reputable distillery. A pager beeps as Pagan pours the battered martinis into glasses. "A CLIENT! I'm broke." He hands me a frothy cocktail.

Pagan examines the pager's LED readout. "657-4501. Hmmmm. Sounds familiar. I wonder if it's a regular." He sits in a rocking chair and sorts through a metal 3x5 card file. "I keep my client cards in order by phone number. 654, 655, 657-0, 657-3...here we go. Stumpy!"

"Stumpy?"

"He's got a plastic leg."

"Does he take it off?"

Pagan picks up the phone. "Sometimes. He stays dressed mostly. All he really wants to do is talk while I walk around in the buff. He's lonely. So many of them are. Excuse me while I call him."

I amuse myself by looking at an extensive collection of adult videos. The men on these boxes are incredibly handsome. Where do they find these bodies? Wouldn't that be a great job: talent scout for some porno producer. Why don't I have a body like this? I'm lazy. I love fried food. Gravy. Don't forget my booze. Oh, well—Barbara Cartland says a gal of a certain age has to choose between her face or her figure. I'll take the face. It's easy. Shoulder pads will camouflage the figure flaws. Pagan hangs up and turns to me. "He'll be here in an hour. Do you want to borrow one?"

"Me? No. I don't have a TV."

"NO TV?!" Pagan exclaims. "How can you LIVE?"

I laugh. I hear this all the time. "Oh, Pagan, really. There's never anything on. Crap. Besides, it forces me to read more."

"I'll bet you jack off a lot."

I choke on a swallow of martini. I do love the unexpected.

"I should get going. Can I bring the glass back tomorrow?"

"Sure." Pagan opens the door with one hand and touches my arm with the other. "I hope what I told you doesn't change anything. I hope you still like me."

"Don't be ridiculous."

I walk into the hallway, carefully balancing my drink as I descend two flights of stairs.

TRICK

"This is a pay-to-play bar. Either you come up with some cash, or we'll send you cryin' back to Orange County."

Perplexed by the sudden change in what was a pleasant conversation, I smile lamely at the young man's attempt to insult me. He turns angrily on his heels and disappears into the crowd.

The concept of the whore with a heart of gold out the window, I look around the room. It's obvious who are the johns and who's the trade. That guy thought I was going to pay? Not on his life. I shouldn't need to do that for a few years yet. I'd guess.

Pagan's story has rekindled my fascination with prostitution. I've never actually turned a trick (Not for cash. I'm not of above putting out for a good meal, however.), but the tawdry idea of earning a living at the expense of some man's fetish is intriguing. Vic and John both paid rent by working for an escort service when we were fresh and young. Their stories titillated and aroused my curiosity. I admired my friends' chutzpah. I could never work up the nerve to ask a person for money. I was a walking charitable institution.

I order a martini from the bartender. I have that glow. This is fun. Turning from the bar, I catch my reflection in a wall of mirrors. The blazer is what fooled that nasty tramp. I'm adorned in john wear. A blazer represents cash flow; T-shirts, a need.

I'm attracting more attention than anticipated. New meat. My goal was to blend in and watch. To take in the scene. To be invisible. I'll just sink into the shadows, over here, by the cigarette machine.

"What's a beauty like you doing in the dark?" The Englishman caught me off guard.

"Just watching."

"I didn't think you were one of the boys. Fascinating, isn't it?"

I nod.

"First time?"

"No." It's been years.

The elderly gent brings a hand to his chin, stroking as he assesses my person. "What's your story? You're not shopping, are you?"

I smile and shake my head. "Negative."

"Are you an undercover cop?"

"Nope."

"I shouldn't think so. You don't seem like a pervert, but you never can tell at first glance." He taps an index finger on his cheek. "I'd guess that you're a writer."

A writer? That's what I get for wearing plaid. I smile but neither confirm or deny.

"What ho!" Pleased with his deduction, the Englishman claps his hands together. Men are so easy.

The nasty tramp leans around a john to glare at me. I'm horning in on the trade.

"That young man seems interested in you."

"Not really. He told me off earlier. Thought I was going to pay."

"Mercenary fellow." The Englishman turns toward me, placing his hand on my crotch. I let him. "It can't be easy trying to make a living as a writer."

"It's not," I lie.

"I think you'll do. I was looking at spending $100 tonight." The Englishman squeezes what is becoming erect. Money has that effect on me.

"For an hour?"

"For one hour."

I've been propositioned. What to do? He's older. Handsome in his way. The accent doesn't hurt the charm factor. God knows I've slept with worse. I think of that check for the landlord I have to write.

What the hell.

CHRISTMAS

I've been drinking for two days. The usual gloom cocktail. Scotch rocks.

Christmas. Bah. Humbug.

I pad to the bar and pour another. Hell. Out of ice. Who needs it? Scotch up! I walk back to the darkened bedroom.

I didn't expect the Christmas edict of Mom's to affect me this way. Oh, I always get a holiday depression, but this year! I am a mess. I've resorted to calling in sick.

The phone rings. Again. Let the machine answer. A hang-up. I don't care.

Down again. Someone pulled the elusive rug of confidence out from under me. It had to happen. I was up for too long. Three months, flying high. Without drugs.

I could use a line.

When did this happen? It just hit me—an Acme anvil falling from the sky. Usually I can see the gray clouds of despair on the horizon. A change in sleep patterns. Nightmares. Loss of appetite. Trembling hands. There was no storm warning this time. Suddenly here I am, the wraith in a robe.

I pick up the phone thinking *I'll call Mom.* Sometimes it helps. I hang up. FUCK HER. She's half the problem. SHE IS THE PROBLEM. Selfish cow. Too afraid of conflict. My brothers have fought for years. It started long ago. She always washed her hands of the responsibility rather than mediating. Too much work, this understanding. Easier to turn a blind eye; the deaf ear.

She was the Amazing Invisible Mom.

Just disappear when there's a conflict. Jump into a book! Go shopping! Now you see her/now you don't! The Amazing Invisible Mom protects HERSELF! The scientists here at Ronco designed her that way. The patented defense mechanism enables the Amazing Invisible Mom to evaporate at a moment's notice! If you order now, we'll send you this Fucked-up Father to complete your foolproof kit to neurosis, nightmares, and nausea! Don't delay! Order yours TODAY.

Where was she? Where? How could she let it happen? Why did she not do what even a cat would do instinctively? The law of the jungle is survival. She chose to survive. She chose to protect herself.

I don't want to think about this.

I kick off the covers and grab my drink from the nightstand. It's Christmas. I amble into the living room and sit near the window. In the empty parking lot below, a little boy rides a bicycle in a wobbly figure eight. First bike. A gift from Santa. He falls. Wiping the dirt from his elbows, the kid climbs back on and starts again. He'll get the hang of it. Always do. I did. By New Year's.

Christmas in my family had nothing to do with kids. None of that lovey-dovey crap. Nah, it was a boozefest. A reason for grown-ups to belt down a few gallons of sauce. A real trailer-trash affair. Dirty jokes. A fight. Some tears. That inbred wife of my walleyed Baptist minister uncle telling Gramma she was a lush.

Dad trying to make nice with the kids after tormenting us all year. "I'm not feeling any animosity." Whoopee. Hot breath of 100 proof making me as queasy as the hairy arms holding me. "You can hug me back, dammit," he'd slur.

I couldn't. I just couldn't.

I freshen my drink. I want to be oblivious. It wouldn't be Christmas without cocktails. One must honor the traditions one knows.

Dad lingers on my mind. Why won't he leave me alone, that bastard.

I walk back to the chair.

I hated that man. The torture. The lies. Nowhere to run. No escape. He'll always find you. Still does—in dreams.

A little boy lays in a bed rocking back and forth, back and forth. He embraces the only thing he has. Himself. He prays. He prays real hard, 'cause if you pray real hard God will hear the lamb and He will find him and He will save him. If you pray real hard this God of Love will make what you want come true.

Please let Dad die
Please let Dad die
Please let Dad die
Please...

A knock at the door. I stop rocking. Who can it be? I rise and walk to the entryway. Maybe it's Momma Scrooge reneging on her edict. "Who is it?"

"Katherine," calls a voice through the door.

"Katie, I'm sick. I look awful. Please go away."

"I am not leaving the building until you open this door."

"Is that an order?"

"What do you think?"

I open the door. Ever cool, Katherine ignores my boozy appearance. "Merry Christmas," I say.

"Merry Christmas," says she. "I'm here to take you out to dinner."

"Katie, I'm so sick."

"I know how you're sick." She points to the iceless glass in my hand. "We all do. We've been worried at the hotel."

Busted.

"I want you to get out of that robe and come with Nicholas and me for Christmas dinner."

"NICHOLAS? You expect me to have dinner with my archrival? Look at me, Katherine! You can't be serious."

"The pity party has begun," Katherine jeers. "Stop being so self-centered. That boy hasn't got a family to call his own in this country. It was his idea to collect you in the first place."

"It was?"

"Yes, it was," she mimics my whiny voice. "Go get in the shower. We'll be back in a half-hour. And don't get any big ideas about disappearing before I get back. We both want you with us for the holiday."

A half-hour. I'll never be ready in time.

NEW YEAR'S EVE

I stand hanging on the pay phone at Crescent Heights and Sunset Boulevard. The Garden of Allah used to be here. Now it's a strip mall.

"Hello?" An answer; he's awake.

"Hey Vic, it's me. Happy New Year."

"Hi, Coif."

"I need a Bloody Mary, wanna come?"

"What time is it?"

"After 9."

"OK."

I walk to the car. The sun streams onto my hungover face. A perfect winter morning. Bright. Crisp. Cool.

Last night, in classic form, I downed numerous martinis in countless bars. I made out with some guy from Seattle at Mother Lode and woke up this morning in the Ramada Beverly Hills with someone else. I discovered the flight attendant in bed with me after gradually realizing: *Home I'm not in*.

I drive along the Sunset Strip. Traffic is mercifully light. I need the hair of the dog, and quick. My head is killing me.

As I pull up to the apartment building, a friendly neighborhood drug dealer whistles. Ignore him. Crack has never thrilled me. The high is too short.

Vic answers the intercom at the security door on my third try. "Marco's asleep. I'll be right down."

I go to the car and put the top down. My mouth tastes disgusting. Vic keeps me waiting for 10 minutes before finally traipsing down the front steps.

"Hi, doll!"

I take the passenger seat, allowing Vic to assume the wheel. I don't want to be in control today. I want a cocktail.

We cruise westward toward Santa Monica. It is a glorious day.

We stop at the Bel Age Hotel and savor our first Mary. From the roof deck there's a spectacular view of the L.A. basin.

"This town can be beautiful."

"Yep."

We head back down Sunset. In the burgundy convertible—Vic in a red beret and me in a brightly printed shirt: It's Fag Patrol! A carload of UCLA students holler "FAIRY" as they pass in Westwood. We laugh.

Vic parks the car in front of the S.S. Friendship, a Santa Monica watering hole. The owner and his staff busily remove Christmas decorations as we poke our heads out of sunlight and into the darkened bar.

"You open?"

"Sure, come on in."

We order a round of drinks. We plant ourselves at a table near the jukebox.

Finally, a buzz. My headache but a memory, Vic and I engage in the nostalgic conversation of old friends as they reach a milestone of longevity.

CRAIG CURTIS

"God…when I was a kid, we had a milkman."

"Us too. Till high school."

"EDGEWOOD!" we cry in unison.

"Remember those ice cream socials?"

"How about the Sadie Hawkins dance? You and that bitch sitting on a haystack."

"Her! Don't remind me. I was so skinny then."

"You've never been SO skinny."

Vic shoots a death glare, then smiles. Introspective, we sit in silence, listening as another CD clicks into place.

"We are the last innocents."

I look down and absorb Vic's statement. The last generation to live simply. Black-and-white TV. Charge-a-plates. Grilled cheese at the counter at Woolworth's. What a big world it was. How simple. How safe.

Nostalgia. Bah.

I was never innocent. I knew what people were capable of before I started kindergarten. It happened in my house. Behind closed doors.

Joy was pilfered early. Happiness…maimed. Though bitter and blighted, I keep wishing for better, hoping for beautiful, and hungry for one elusive thing I've never understood. Love.

What a fool.

I catch myself staring, as I so often have, into the open mouth of the glass before me. Ice cubes float in liquid as red and viscous as my tainted blood.

I will spend this New Year's Eve in solitude.

Alone in my apartment, I listen to phone messages while laying down for a nap. Calls from friends inquiring about plans for the evening. One from Katherine, worried. The flight attendant called from Dallas. Finally, a message from the man I made out with at Mother Lode. I scarcely remember him.

Oh, my head.

I think of the last message as I drift off to sleep. Tomorrow I will call him back. Maybe this time it will work out.

OUTED

The pig is promising me a gift. I want cash. Or at least a clari-fication on "gift." The expensive Swiss timepiece on his wrist would do.

"You're no whore," he keeps telling me. I don't know whether to be flattered or insulted.

"I've been paid," I tell him indignantly.

This pig would want to pay me. He's gruesome. The only rea-son I climbed into this car is because I'm very drunk. It's a Bentley. What the hell.

The pig grabs my head and wrenches my face toward his. He leans into me, kissing hard.

"You BIT me!" I cry, pushing away.

The pig leers. He's rich. Taking liberties is a way of life.

I'm not sure how to escape or what to do. I never attended that course with Pagan. Prostitution II: How to Divert a Freak. I've only learned how much to charge per hour.

I look past the pig toward my car parked merely spaces away. It seems like miles. With my poor and drunken eyesight, I can dis-cern a figure hovering about the convertible. I'd swear it was a straight man.

SPENCER!

I push the pig off me and lurch from the car. This scoop is far more important than a folly of degradation for a token of gratitude.

"Spencer, DAH-ling," I call in my finest Preston/Tallulah bellow. "What are YOU doing in the ALLEY?"

The alley is a well-known gay cruising spot off of Santa Monica Boulevard, behind a bar and an adult bookstore. It is not the kind of place in which heterosexual men prefer to find themselves after dark. It is a bastion of cheap sex.

Eyes like hubcaps on the car I've just escaped from, Spencer searches for a logical lie. An explanation for the highly unusual predicament his breeder self is in. "I, uh, uh, well, er...I GOT A TICKET! Yeah, for running a stop sign. I was so upset that I had to pull over, and, well, here I am. Quite embarrassing, I must say." He points to my car. "I thought maybe you were nearby." Spencer smiles sheepishly. "Kind of a lot of activity here, wouldn't you say?"

"I would say," I smirk. "You may as well come clean, doll. I know about you."

Spencer laughs nervously. He's caught. Arms crossed, I lean against the hood of the car, tapping my foot expectantly.

"How long have you known?"

"Since about 15 minutes after we met, you silly thing." I pat Spencer on the padded shoulder of his navy jacket. "Sometimes people recognize a bit of themselves in others."

"I thought you found out about that guest."

"You slept with a HOTEL GUEST?!"

Spencer tells the story of a handsome translator for a European symphony conductor. Nicholas and I both lusted openly for the man, whispering like schoolgirls whenever he was in the lobby.

"How was it?" I ask.

"Big butt, little dick."

"Spoken like a true fag."

A scrawny man with a crew cut walks over, interested in one or both of us. "Hey."

"Hey," I echo.

"What are you guys up to?"

"Well, my straight friend here just got a traffic ticket."

"How long ago?"

"About 45 minutes," Spencer replies.

"I'm a cop. Maybe I can help you out."

I'm skeptical. "Help him? How?"

"Let me see the ticket."

Spencer reaches into the breast pocket of his jacket and produces a flimsy pink rectangle of paper. I am stunned to find that the ticket story is true.

"Hey, this was written by Aguirre. He's a buddy of mine. If this thing's not on the roster yet, I could probably get it lost."

"Really?!" Spencer exclaims delightedly.

"Sure. It will cost 20 bucks to deprocess it, though."

Spencer pays the man.

"Could you give me a lift to the station?"

We climb into Spencer's car and drive to the West Hollywood precinct. The cop tells us he will be 10 minutes. We talk as we wait. Spencer is as eager to chat as I am to listen.

"It's my family, you see. I was raised Irish Catholic."

"Say no more."

"It's not the religious question. It's something deeper. A sense that I'm dishonoring the family name with this deviance. There is a tremendous amount of expectation coming from my background. A code of responsibility. An adherence to the laws of a society that predates the Gilded Age." Spencer sighs. "Homosexuals are irrelevant; inconsequential, where I come from."

"Hairdressers?"

Spencer laughs. "It's just the feeling that I'm letting my family and friends down with this perversion." A pause. "I don't want to be inconsequential."

"Spencer, your attitudes toward your sexuality are medieval, for chrissake. Your family is on the other coast. They'll never need to know unless you tell them. As far as your friends here are concerned, well, this is California. Do you think anyone gives a flying hoo-ha who you fuck? Come on, man."

Spencer looks away, staring into the park across San Vicente Boulevard. "I'm just so ashamed."

We sit quietly. I search for something to say.

"I understand your shame. Not for your sexuality, so much, but I do know what it's like to keep dark secrets. To have to lie to protect who you are." I stop. I am uncomfortable with the truth. "Spencer, you have to stop lying and accept yourself." Abruptly I change the subject. "Hey, where the hell is that guy?! We've been waiting an hour."

"Do you think we've been taken?" Spencer asks.

"Yeah, I think we've been taken. That guy was too skinny to be a cop."

"I can't believe it! I gave that man 20 dollars! I can't believe I was so stupid to fall for this ploy. It's despicable." Spencer starts the car.

"You know, Spencer, this is a case in point."

"Why are you laughing?"

"A couple of charlatans hoodwinked by a snake in the grass.

You'd think one of us would be sophisticated enough to see it. Like, I haven't lived in the city for more than two days."

"I lived in Manhattan! You're not going to tell anyone about this gay thing, are you?"

"Never."

I'm lying.

SEATTLE

"I love you."

I look at the man who said it. Love. Me? After three weeks of phone conversation? I didn't even recognize him at the airport.

"Can I kiss you?"

I let him. Why not. He paid for my plane fare.

The kiss is rigid. Stiff. This will be no make-out session. Not like at Mother Lode. I'm sober.

I am uncomfortable with the revelation. It is shocking. How can he love me? He knows nothing of me. Nothing except what I've told him, which is nothing, to be sure. Nothing of my past. Nothing of my present. Nothing of my future.

I must tell him. I'm tired of lying.

At dinner I talk of my childhood. A little. Almost nothing. A dim illumination onto a warped psychology. The psychology of the guy he "loves."

He finishes his salad. He pushes the plate away. He wipes a dribble of bleu cheese dressing from his chin. He looks at me blankly, wondering.

"No matter," he says. "It's nothing."

In bed, I warn of something as he turns off the light.

"I talk—sometimes."

"Talk?"

"In my sleep. Nightmares."

"Oh. I see. No matter."

It's nothing.

I lie in the dark at the edge of the bed. Perhaps, I muse, he is the man for me. Perhaps he is The One.

I wake suddenly. A shudder. Two eyes stare down. He's watching.

"You're cute. I love your hair."

"It's fake. I color it."

"No matter."

In the chill of early morning, we walk to Pike's Market. We eat cinnamon rolls from a stand. Seattle coffee warms me.

"You know, I've had a drug problem. In the past." I'm saying something. He listens. He eats his pastry. He licks the frosting from his fingertips. He drinks his coffee.

"No matter. It's nothing. I love your tan."

"It's fake," I tell him.

"No matter."

We drive out of the city. He plays a Doris Day tape. We both know the songs. We sing.

The falls are beautiful. Inspiring. Scenic. He brushes my hand with his. He wants to hold it, but he can't. Not here. Not now. Not in public. I lean against the railing and tell of my disenchantment with romance. Of a bitterness instilled in me by men afraid of my information. I'm saying something. Of my past.

I tell of my fear of intimacy.

"It's nothing. No matter. They filmed *Twin Peaks* here."

The weekend ends too quickly. We sit in the car at the airport.

We hold hands. I have one more secret. One more toadstool. One more horror. The big one. The future.

"I'm HIV-positive."

"No matter. It's nothing."

The answer is concise, Strong. It's nothing.

"I've been talking all weekend. Is there anything you'd like to say?"

He thinks for a minute and shakes his head. "I can't think of anything. No. Nothing."

I sit at a window on the plane. I watch as the last pieces of baggage are loaded into the compartment beneath the floor. I told the truth. I've said something. Can he be The One? Could I let him love me? Can I love him back? Will I now begin to understand what has eluded me before?

No matter.

LOVELY DAY FOR A MASSACRE, DARLING

Quel désastre!

My slippers stick to the cocktail scunge on the kitchen floor. Nasty. Looks like the Royal Lippizaner Stallions trudged through here. Cigarette butts float in one of my good glasses. I hate that. This is why I don't throw parties very often. The mess.

My first annual February 14th Soiree was a success. I don't know how many people showed. More than expected. Most single. I wanted that. A night of celebration for those of us without Valentines.

There were, naturally, a few guests with dates. What could I do? Throw them out? Singles only. Get out, and take your cheesy date widdya. It didn't take long for them to weed themselves out. Most couples stopped in to have a drink, say hello, and then skip off to do whatever it is those people *do* do on a romantic holiday. *The* romantic holiday. A day to line the pockets of florists and chocolatiers with gold.

The dining room floor is coated with a layer of *hors d'oeuvres* debris. Bits of cheesecake. More cigarette butts. I couldn't empty ashtrays fast enough. It seems that everyone smoked as much as they drank. The apartment smells like a stale saloon.

I walk to the living room and open another window. My throat is killing me. One too many smokes. The oral aerobics with Nicholas don't help. Drunk, we did the bad thing in the bedroom (with a living room full of guests). That's what happens when ice cubes of contempt melt into a cocktail of mutual admiration. Two narcissists finding what they love about themselves in another. Sadly, Nicholas is not boyfriend material. He shares my penchant for men with wallets. How will I face him at work?

My damn head. I drank everything that was handed to me. Maybe some aspirin will help?

On the way to the bathroom, I stop in the dressing chamber. These handprints! My landlord is going to kill me.

I dragged each guest in on arrival and dipped their right hand into tempera paint. If the drug addicts on the street didn't surprise them, this handprint ritual did. Each print was then signed by the owner in marking pen. My towels are ruined from the cleanup. I'll never get my security deposit back. Who cares? The wall looks great.

"Give him a hand!" wrote Katie. She's responsible for the cheesecake carpeting. Dahlia opted for the classic signature and date. She turned up with a surfer on one arm and a Spaniard on the other. Two escorts! Spencer salivated openly over the surfer, while Preston cornered the dazzling Spaniard, conversing with him in his native tongue. The gypsy Preston, I will learn tomorrow, walked out with a drink in his hand, depleting my set of glasses to three. Terry sang Cole Porter a cappella. His print was made into a Thanksgiving turkey. He was accompanied by a blond Brazilian, whose name I forget and whose signature is illegible. Also accompanying Terry was Danny, the most conversational of guests. He discussed Proust with Katherine and played

coy with Pagan, who signed each of his five fingers with a different misnomer. Pagan made the entrance of the night (very late)
wearing an Indian sari and a behemoth red Afro wig. Also in
house were Vic and Marco, who brought along a makeup artist
with a Madonna fixation, and an actor who shall remain name-
less but not without signature—it's the largest on the wall. He
stood around (as actors do) espousing the merits of Strasberg, to
which Vic suggested that all Studio alumni were on par with Sally
Kirkland. The actor left shortly thereafter. The most interesting
print belongs to a neighborhood gang member, his signature
printed in the cursive of thugs. He was uninvited, but no trouble,
so we took a vote and he stayed. At 3 A.M. the party was still going
strong.

I wash down aspirin with a slug of water.

This is fulfillment. In only short months I've gotten it together. I am the person I want to be. To think of where I was!

Yet one thing is missing. That dirge of poets. What we are
raised to believe is the fruit of life. The reason this holiday exists.

I count the prints. 27 hands. Scarlet. For the occasion.
February 14th, Valentine's Day.

SEATTLE

"I think you should call in sick."

My third visit to the Northwest at his expense. I'm flying out on the last possible plane, in time for my evening shift at the concierge desk.

Things are heating up. He wants a commitment. He wants to "marry" me.

"Just like those guys in that book," he repeats. I'm getting the hard sell. "I just don't want a long-distance relationship anymore. It's not working for me."

It is working for me.

I look at the man, puzzled. Calling in sick is no big deal. No job ever interfered with my personal life. But to pack on a whim (his), sell my shit, quit my job, and move to this godforsaken land of garage bands and computer nerds? The constant rain? The weather is as chilling as the rented furniture he lives with. The Nagel print above that black dresser! Ugh. This shit's gotta go. I wonder at the lack of family pictures. The vacuum of personality.

"It's only furniture," he says. "If you move up, you can do whatever you want with the house."

"What about the cottage cheese ceiling?"

"There's only so much you can do with corporate housing. Besides, the home office pays the rent. Beggars can't be choosers."

A cliché. How delightful.

The current status of the tryst is working for me. I'm very free to do what I want, providing I'm home by 11 when he calls to make sure I'm there, which I am not always, but he deals with it, because, I don't really care, because, he's a couple of thousand miles and two states away and there's only so much one can do through fiber optics so crystal clear you can hear a heart drop.

"I haven't dated anyone since we met," he says stupidly. "Have you?"

I lie. Why tell him the truth? I haven't become emotionally attached to anyone, if that's what he means. Certainly no one else has gifted me as extravagantly as has he. I don't really want to date. No commitments. I'm having too much fun.

"We will be so happy, I promise. I love you."

"I love you too." I think. Oh, hell!

The man snuggles closer to me. I'm suffocating under this down comforter. I stare at the fucking ceiling, thinking about the new development. An adventure. A new town. Security?

"What about work?"

"No problem! The rent's free. You won't have to worry about a thing. I make enough to provide for us both. I can take care of you. All you need to do is be here and look after your health." He pushes a porous snatch of bang from my eyes. "No one's ever loved you like I can love you. Taking care of you—that's what it's about."

Now he's talking.

"See, you don't know what love is. You couldn't—after all you told me about your childhood. People like you have to be taught what it is to be loved. To be trained. I can train you. I can take care of you. Only I can love you."

He's right I presume. What he says makes sense. I never learned it. There's something wrong with me. Always was. I need to be tutored. To be taught.

"I don't know." I look over at the man doing the number on my psyche. He stares hopefully. Compelling me. Buying me. Not the finest-looking chap I've ever known. Curious George with a flat top. Weak chin. Ears like Gable. Well, there's something, I guess. Shallow me. It's time I grow up and realize that looks ain't everything. Why couldn't I love a man for his innards? Why?

We kiss. "Marry me," he whispers. "Only I can love you."

I point to the phone on the bed stand beside him. "Hand me that."

He smiles.

I hope I'm making the right decision.

DAHLIA

"I hope you thought this thing through. It doesn't seem like you've known him long enough."

Dahlia and I walk from the gallery onto Wilshire Boulevard. Most disconcerting to have this conversation as Picasso's women weep. Hushed tones of urgency in the museum. How utterly dramatic.

"I don't have a choice now, Dahlia. My fate is sealed."

"What option did you give us? Everyone KNEW you were in Seattle when you called in. Then to show up two hours late the next day! You were really pushing it."

"My plane was delayed?"

"Is that why you were drunk?"

"No, I was drunk because the dashing flight attendant fancied me and presented me with a full bottle of Cabernet from first class." Triumphantly I add, "Plus a REAL glass, with stem."

We stop to wait for the signal to change at Fairfax.

"Let me understand this. You felt compelled to drink a full bottle of wine because you had a real *glass*?"

"It was a two-and-a-half-hour flight." We cross the street.

A most humane dismissal, this firing. "It breaks my heart to have to do this," said the personnel director (Dahlia's boss). "You leave us no choice."

I sat numbly listening as staff members wandered around outside the office, gossiping. *What's happening? Are they really going to give him the shaft? I heard they were preparing the check at lunch. He's so nice but kind of dumb* and all the usual crap as the ax fell. No Ifs, Ands, or Buts. I signed the document in triplicate and graciously accepted the check that had in fact been prepared earlier in the day, and, with as much pride as I could muster (HUGE grin), walked out through the front doors of the Brentwood Duquessa for the first and last time. NO employee entrance for this departing staff member, hell no!

INSUBORDINATION.

I've been insubordinate before. I'm not sure what plain-old subordination is. I've been fired before too. Never felt a thing. Just made my patented exit and didn't look back.

This time it's different.

We walk into the coffee shop. The waitress smiles. She knows me. I eat here.

"How are you?"

"Fine, thanks." I wave away the menu she offers. "I know what I want."

Dahlia and I resume our conversation after ordering.

"If you hadn't been so flippant, they may have only reprimanded you."

"Flippant?"

"The outfit, for one."

"So I wore an ascot, big deal."

"Very theatrical," Dahlia says, posturing hammily.

"Well, it doesn't matter now. I'm history."

"You most certainly are. You're history."

I sip iced tea. I wish it were something stronger.

Humiliation singes gossamer pride. Latent self-respect. The Brentwood Duquessa was pivotal in finding strength. I saw the ad in the *Times*. I knew the position was mine. I walked in and claimed it. It belonged to me. I have, as effectively as I conquered it, destroyed it. This rape and pillage is growth. I think. I'm sacrificing a career for what I've always longed for. It's worth it.

Isn't it?

"If you think you're doing the right thing, then I'm happy for you. I just hope you realize that relationships aren't always what they're cracked up to be." Dahlia rearranges flatware on the paper napkin in front of her. "Look at what happened to me."

She continues after a mournful silence. "If things don't work out for whatever reason, you know you can always come home. I'll help you out, if I can."

X-ray eyes pierce the façade. Stop looking at me!

"I appreciate it, Dahlia, really. He's a good man. I know it's going to work out. I know it is."

SEX

"Pose for me."

I stand naked. What exactly does He mean, "pose"? Should I flex? Should I jack off? What? Reminds me of the time I entered a "talent" contest at an adult theater in San Francisco. Teetering at the end of a catwalk, blinded by a spotlight, thinking: *I'm broke. I'm pathetic. My life has come to this?* I lost but got 10 bucks for showing all to an audience of faceless, panting men. This audience has a face.

"It's because of your illness," He tells me. "We have to be careful."

Intimacy is not an option. I don't argue. He pays the bills.

While I'm posing He whips out old pencilis erectus. Woo-hoo. When He's finished I get dressed. Or go to bed. Doesn't matter.

"Can't we just make love?"

"What's wrong with you?!" He barks. "It's because of YOU we can't. I have to be careful."

He pays the bills.

The rule of caution is variable. After a fight we are intimate. After bickering we make love. Then He'll get naked. Then He'll be close. Then He'll stick it to me. I lay facedown, teeth clenched on a pillow, quills jabbing my palate. A few crude strokes, and it's over. The argument's won.

And He thought I didn't know what love is.

MIDDLE CLASS

"It's embarrassing how conservative my sister is. I mean, she shops at Crate and Barrel, she likes ethnic stuff. But she's *so* right-wing!"

I smile at the lady on my left and nod before burying myself in the menu. As if Republicans don't shop at the mall.

"What are you going to have?" asks the lady across from me.

"I'm not sure." I look at the evening's selections from the chef's "Northwest Cuisine" kitchen. I see bearnaise. I see hollandaise. Caesar Salad. Fusilli pasta. What on this menu is indigenous to the region? O-o-oh. Salmon. A-a-ah. Lingon berries. Gentrified lumberjack food. After having eaten in the fine bistros of L.A., I find it hard to compare this very common hotel-dining-room fare to anything remotely eclectic. Seattle's pride in itself escapes me. Of course they do have COFFEE but god knows the beans are imported. I think the dollop of steamed milk floating in it comes from cattle native to the area. I don't know any cows personally, or I'd ask.

"How are you enjoying Seattle compared to *California?*" asks the lady on my left.

"I love it," I lie.

"You're from CALIFORNIA!" exclaims the lady across from me. "Miserable place. How can you *admit* to being from there?"

I look down the long table at Him as He anguishes over what wine to order. He sits with His buddies, while I have been banished to the hausfrau corner. He looks up from the list at me then back to his friends. "*The Vine Dictator* says that this Chardonnay is an excellent vintage. Grassy, oaky, buttery, with a finish of springtime."

Trumped-up commercial chatter. Sounds like a convergence of fragrance models.

The waitress serves me a martini—boozy, turpentiney, with a finish of bedtime. I'm far enough away from Him to rebel against His dictates. His glare from down the table says it all. THAT'S IT. THAT'S THE ONLY ONE. YOU KNOW HOW YOU GET WHEN YOU DRINK.

I hold up the mutinous glass in mock salute. "To chronic drizzle." We clink glasses. The sarcasm is ignored.

I order filet mignon.

"Red MEAT!" cries the lady on my left.

"It will kill you," agrees the lady across from me.

"But it's good!" I protest. "What did you order?" I call to Him.

"The lemon prawn pasta."

Why ask? A creature of habit. It's always the same: pasta topped with chicken or shrimp, preceded by a salad with extra bleu cheese dressing. His taste in food is as exotic as His taste in friends.

I find myself in a conversation of letters. Seattle proudly buys more books per capita than any other city in the nation. I'd never have known this factual twaddle except that it is a sampling of the propaganda put out by the Seattle Chamber of Commerce in order to make citizens feel a bit better about living. Here. John Grisham's latest judicial pulp is the literary lingo tonight.

"Are YOU reading right now?" asks the lady on my left.

I am.

"What is it?"

"*A Tree Of Night and Other Stories* by Truman Capote."

The lady across frowns. "He was a weirdo."

I order another martini. He glares. I drink.

Next, a stimulating conversation on film. Seattle-ites love to bitch-bitch-bitch about L.A., but—if they'd put their money where their mouths are—they'd stop spending more per capita on what is an import from the hellish land they loathe. Dark theaters are far more comfortable than dank outdoors. The cinematic plight of a bus rigged with explosives fuels the wagging of tongues.

"I didn't see it."

"What have you seen?" asks the lady on my left.

Having not seen a movie in a while (He and I don't agree on what is entertainment), I talk of a play called *Holiday Heart*.

"Sounds cute," says the lady on my left.

"A drama about a transvestite and a crack addict, of all things," disapproves the lady across. "I read it in the paper."

"Oh, dear," says the lady to the left. "I go to the show to be ENTERTAINED."

"As do I," agrees the lady across.

The conversation takes another turn. Having nothing to add to the discussion, I lose myself in the salad. It seems that strollers now have three wheels, and Nike has replaced Keds. Cream-of-mushroom soup is a constant, however. It is still the main ingredient in many a one-dish meal.

I ponder all of my thrashing about. The experimentation. The struggle. For what? To find myself in the northernmost outpost of

West Covina? Oh, Seattle gives itself airs. Big city. Urbane. You can replace crumbled potato chips with french-fried onions and call it gourmet, but a casserole is a casserole is a casserole.

The server sets the entrée in front of me.

"That looks delicious," says the lady across, "for beef."

"What is it that you do for work?"

"My laundry," He interjects blithely.

We all laugh.

CROSSFIRE

ME: You don't think that film sent out all kinds of warped messages to the audience?

HIM: Messages? What? It was just a movie.

ME: It was just a movie that said, Be a moron, do what you're told, and you can be a war hero, an Olympic champion, meet presidents, get money—let's see, what else...

HIM: You're stupid. Shut up and eat.

ME: Oh, yeah. All the usual stuff about women.

HIM: What?

ME: The mother prostitutes herself for the son.

HIM: She loved him. She wanted him to get an education.

ME: Bro-ther. How about the girlfriend? A coke whore. Oh, yes! Hollywood's come a long way baby.

HIM: Shut up and eat.

ME: You talk to me. What did you think?

HIM: I liked it. It made me feel real nice.

ME: You're a chump. Rhymes with...

HIM: I know what it rhymes with. You just think you're so smart, dontcha. Well I'm sick of talking about everything. It was just a MOVIE! It didn't MEAN anything. It said NOTHING. You should say as much as that flick.

ME: You're right of course. It said nothing INTENTIONALLY. It was just a jack-off show for Industrial Light and Magic.

HIM: What?

ME: The company that did the special effects. There was certainly *nothing* to the plot. But the themes. I can't stop thinking about what Lillian Gish said about the power of cinema.

HIM: Who?

ME: Shut up and eat.

BEG ME

He looks at me, incredulous. Angry. As if I'd stabbed him with a hat pin.

"I can't believe I'm HEARING this! I can't believe it! After ALL I've done for you."

He's bluffing, unwilling to part with any of the dollars He earns for anything other than what He feels is important. My eyesight is not a priority. Nor is it His responsibility.

I need a pair of glasses. The headaches are getting worse.

"I'm aware of all that you've done for me. All the plane fares. All the dinners out. I appreciate it. But I need glasses, honey." I drop the top of my shorts, exposing a frayed elastic band. "My underwear is shot."

He crosses His arms. "You have nerve, that's all I can say."

I'm holding my tongue. I have been for the last three months. Controlling myself. Overlooking the constant reminders of my position as His boyfriend. His meager expectations of me. Of my role as Silent Spouse: to be paraded around on a leash. The less I say, the better.

"What do you think it entails—taking care of someone?

WHAT? I don't ask for money very often, and when I do I have to cause a fucking scene. If you had a cat that was sick, wouldn't you take it to the vet?"

"I don't like cats," He snips.

"A MOOT POINT!" This asshole argues like a sixth-grader. I breathe, attempting to maintain a level of civility. The slightest display of emotion will quash any chance of perfecting my vision. "I appreciate that you feed me, but don't forget that I cook the food you bring home. Your company pays the rent here, so the living for two is as cheap as it is for one. I don't ask for much—YOU KNOW THAT. But I have other needs than just food and shelter."

"I know. Why do you think I pay for your highlights? Why do you think I pay for your tanning salon membership? Not to mention the *gym.*"

"Who insists on my looking like goddamn Malibu Ken?"

"Well I don't."

"So if I sat around here and got fat and pale and mousy-brown, it would be okey-dokey-smokey?"

"No matter."

"Yeah, right. You love me for my MIND, I forgot."

He brings an index finger to His chin. "Beg me."

"What!"

"I didn't stutter. Beg."

I begged.

Satiated, He brings me up from my knees, cradling me in His arms. "You shall have your glasses," He says, stroking my hair. "You shall see again." He lifts my face to His. "Would you consider contacts?"

Dazedly victorious, I lean against His bony chest, heavy arms hanging at my sides.

"You know, you can hug me back."
I can't. I just can't.

JOHN

I got the call today.

"He's dead."

"How?"

"Puh-le-e-eze, Coif!" Vic exclaims. "How do you think?"

Overdose. Collapsed. Heart stopped. Cold.

John. Dead.

I don't know if it's shock or what. I don't feel a thing. Maybe I expected it. I don't know.

The John I knew in high school died years ago. The John wrapped up in the drug thing, well, he died that night in handcuffs. For me. Drove away. Never looked back.

"What's with you?" He asks at dinner.

"John's dead."

"Who?" He stares at the TV screen.

"John. My drug friend. He's dead. Vic called today."

Vanna turns four E's. "I hope you're not running up the phone bill."

"I said HE called ME!"

I collect soiled plates and forks and walk to the kitchen. While doing the dishes I think: *It could have been me*.

I walk to the bedroom and slip on a robe.

It is impossible to concentrate tonight. This book holds no interest for me. John. Cold. I pull the blankets up to my chin.

John.

If only you could have seen him stride through the halls in his letterman's jacket. A big E for Edgewood emblazoned on his breast. Puffed with the arrogance of youth. One of the elite. He had good hair, perfectly feathered back from a center part. Yellow. Proud.

Things changed after graduation. He couldn't make the big leagues. He tried. How hard John tried. Playing ball was his dream. His single goal. That was what he had: a dream and good hair.

Ambiguous sexuality didn't help matters. John soon found that he was just a loser. A faggot. Like the skinny guys he used to flick with a wet towel in the locker room. Like me. A sissy who couldn't cut it for the big leagues. A Nothing. A Nobody. Good hair doesn't go too far outside the Public School System. When he hung the jacket in the closet for the last time, he left his pride in the pocket. A letter don't mean much in the real world. It ends up hanging in the dark, a feast for moths. A keepsake. A memory.

John died then.

"What are you thinking about?" He asks.

"Nothing." I kiss Him. "I wonder if I have a story in me? I wonder if I could write?"

He yawns and rolls over, facing the wall. He plumps a pillow before thunking His head into it. "You should write for TV. That's where the money is." He switches off the lamp.

Thoughts of John pulse through my head. A big stupid laugh.

The toss of good hair. Haunting me. Why don't I feel anything? Why can't I cry?

His breathing becomes rhythmic beside me. Heavy. Relaxed. He snores softly.

I sneak out of the bedroom. I search through the desk for a yellow pad. I light a candle. Seems fitting for remembrance. Appropriate for lament. I write in a stream of black ink. A steady stream of tears courtesy of Bic pens:

His future was golden, like his hair. Or so he thought.

LIFE

"Your T-cell count has fallen to 80."

I echo the doctor in monotone. "Eighty."

I don't know what else to say. Oh, great! It's finally here! The day I officially got that AIDS diagnosis! After ignoring my health for six months and not taking any drugs as prescribed, what could I expect? A miraculous recovery?

"A count this low legally defines you as having AIDS."

"I know." I look at the speckled tile on the floor. I hate this stuff. An industrial holdover from the '50s. Can't escape it. Even in this podunk town.

A fine film of fog forms on the inside of my glasses.

"I'm also concerned about your weight loss. Seven pounds in a month. Is your appetite OK?"

I remove the glasses from my face. They are no longer aiding my vision.

The doctor slides a box of Kleenex into my lap. "Do you want to talk?"

I'm strangling, grasping, fumbling for decorum to quell the flood, but it won't. Stop. It won't. Stop. Because. It's a long time coming, and he's basically a stranger and, strangely, it's easier to cry in front of a stranger than in front of someone you know. You know? I know it sounds strange, but stranger things happen.

Don't they?

I begin to babble. I've begun to babble to mask my embarrassment at the stupid tears I'm shedding over what I am not sure of it's just bigger than I imagined and (forgive me but) I'm dying and I'm dying in a province where they HATE us Californians and I'M from California and (forgive what I was saying but) the man who is the money, well, he told me that he loved me and at first it was elation, then he mocked my information and it's now humiliation—no! it feels like degradation (all this verbal contemplation; I need a head examination), the game is called intimidation, it's the gist of my starvation. I just can't eat.

"I'm rhyming, aren't I?"

"You are."

"Stupid habit," I mumble through tissue.

"Do you always do that?"

"Do what?"

"Hide behind a burlesque of buffoonery."

A slap? Did this doctor slap me? I haven't been slapped by a doctor since the day I was born. Stunned silence answers the question more eloquently than words.

"Sounds like you're in a bad situation."

I nod. I can't say anything else. If I do, all hell will break loose. Again.

"I'm not a counselor. I am a medical doctor. I can't tell you what to do. However, I can say that this is your *life* we're talking about. When a patient of mine loses seven pounds in a matter of weeks due to stress, I have reason to be concerned. With AIDS eating is living. It's important that you keep your weight up. Not to mention the emotional strain of the relationship you've just described. It's a deadly scenario. Stress oftentimes causes a dramatic drop in T-cells."

A lecture. How soothing to have some respected person tell you all the things you already know.

"I'm dog-paddling, doctor. To keep my head above water."

"Well, it doesn't sound like living to me. How much time do you give to something when time is not yours to give?"

I walk to the bus stop chanting it over and over. WHEN TIME IS NOT YOURS TO GIVE; WHEN TIME IS NOT YOURS TO GIVE.

I look up into curious eyes of azure. Oh, shit. Was I talking to myself again? These bloodshot eyes! Always when there's a cute guy around. He must think I'm the village lunatic.

I climb on the bus and sit near a window. Blue Eyes sits beside me. Right beside me. How much shock can a system take before finally breaking down?

A sturdy leg rubs mine. Our shoulders touch. I don't care. It feels like Life.

He leans across me to pull a cord signaling the driver to stop. His face is close. His warmth. His breath. The moist fragrance of sweet mint. Scent of Life.

Bus stops. He stands. Doors open. Beautiful eyes of blue flash one last look. Beckoning.

What commitment?

A pocketful of free clinic condoms is a good omen. I yell "BACK DOOR" at the driver and dash off the bus.

What the hell.

DEAR AUTHOR

Dear Author,

I have read your story, GOLDEN, as submitted by a mutual acquaintance, Vic Masterson. He is a respected member of our staff. When he came to me last week and asked if I would read a story by a friend of his "to see if it shows promise," I groaned. How many dreary stories do you think cross my desk here? As Editor I don't read stories of friends of friends as a rule. Vic was persuasive. He said he thought it had an edge that would be appreciated by our readership. It does. I couldn't put it down.

I would be interested in running GOLDEN in the coming months. You will be compensated for your effort. Further, we are doing a travel issue in the fall and I was wondering if you would like to contribute something on the Pacific Northwest?

Please contact me with any questions or objections.

Sincerely,
EDITOR IN CHIEF

P.S. Any plans on returning to Los Angeles?

HIM: What's this?

ME: What's it look like? An acceptance letter! They want to buy my first story! Isn't it exciting?!

HIM: See, I told you you should write for TV. What's for dinner?

BOURGEOIS

"It *is* beautiful, isn't it!" Blond proudly gestures around himself. "But really, we overextended ourselves, financially, with the purchase of this house. We were expecting the royalties to be more forthcoming."

"But the book's a hit." I don't know why. Weren't Dick and Jane dull the first time.

"Yes, we did have a hit," Blond replies, "but best-sellers are a one-time thing. No film sale on this book, unfortunately." Smiling, he adds: "Now we devote our time to The Institute."

Brunet strides over. The better half. A washed-up medaled athlete and his bimbo trophy wife. The gay community's version of Frank Gifford and Kathie Lee. Just as upstanding and saccharine sweet. Graduates of the Fags Are Just Like Everybody Else school of thought.

"Are you telling all our ugly secrets?"

Blond twitters as Brunet plays grab-ass with his muscled posterior. How well I know those buttocks. They hang over bars in gay saloons all over the nation. Writer *and* model! Multi-talented, these two. Nudie shots by prominent photographers in hardbound volumes look rather like soft-core pornography to me. If Wegman can dress dogs and call it Art, why can't these clowns disrobe and do the same? They sell plenty of books, if that's what you call them.

Nauseated from the billing and cooing, I walk away thirsty for another beer. He notices me at the cooler and gives me the WE DON'T DRINK DEAR glare. *Fuck* Him.

Perhaps I've died and gone to purgatory. Surely someone would have told me. This fund-raiser needs some real booze to liven things up. Revelers with pulses? These people have Wallets and pristine credit, else they wouldn't have been invited to give generously to The Institute. The Cause. Celebrity Chairmen of a Charitable Foundation. Tax-free dollars. Paychecks.

I have nothing to give. I offer my time. "Do you really think you're our image?" Blond asks. Fuck him.

I barge into a conversation. I have largely been ignored as being someone's boyfriend. HIS. Architect lectures on the wonders of Northwest Architecture. That damn word again. *Northwest.* What can he mean? Totem poles? Log cabins?

"You're including the Sears Catalog shanties and all of Bellevue, I presume."

Architect freezes me with a silent stare. What a bitch. I giggle giddily. I'm just someone's tippling pixie, after all. Someone's boyfriend. HIS.

He pulls me away by the crook of the arm. He warns me to behave. He'd whack me on the nose with a rolled newspaper if He could find one. A muzzle would work. I wrestle free and tramp into the living room.

Pianist punches out Sondheim tunes. Isn't it rich? At least I don't have to talk in here. This room would send Martha Stewart into a fit of apoplexy.

I'm hot. I'm drunk. I'm insulted. I'm bored. The room is tasteless. A gilded coffee table sends me over the edge. The music. The decoration. The conversation. The beer.

I break into a sweat.

My descent into madness. The voices. Telling me. Taunting me. Do it. Do it.

DO IT.

" '*Mabuhay*' *means* '*HELLO*' *in the Philippines!*" I sing a little ditty from last night's Miss Universe Pageant. Live, from Manila, *mabuhay!*

The sudden outburst brings the expected reaction. Music stops. Discussions cease. Heads turn. I laugh.

He's angry. He brings His pocket-pen-protected-self over and announces our departure. I laugh.

"Is he OK?" Blond asks charitably.

"The wifey is fine. He's drunk."

I stop laughing. The wifey!

In the car He berates me for my insolent behavior; Embarrassing not only for Him, but for myself as well. I look out of the window thinking: I hate Him. More than anything.

I deserve it.

When you sell out you get what you're paid for.

IN FLIGHT

"Four dollars, please."

I pay the flight attendant from cash I took from "His" wallet. If you want to hurt an accountant, hit him below the belt: in the pocketbook.

I hit him above the belt, too. A few good swings to the face. That felt good. I expected to hash it out, a real humdinger of a fight. I knew I'd get my ass beat (I punch like a girl; he's taller and 30 pounds heavier), but I didn't care. I had to stand up for myself. For once.

A funny thing happened after I slugged him. The look on his face. *Sur-prise!* Then he turned, ran to the bedroom, jumped in bed, and pulled the covers over his head! He got under the covers and hid away, quaking. I never knew that if you stood up to a bully you'd find a quivering coward beneath the blankets. If only someone had enlightened me before. I would have stood up to Dad. But then I was a kid.

Now I am a man. A delirious fop of a man, complete with demons and holy grail. Next time I set out on a quest for love, I'll go to the pound and adopt a cat.

So. I'm returning home in the face of a breakup. Danger. Family. Loneliness. Crystal. Illness. Ambivalence. Distrust. Danger. Home.

I don't want to think about this.

I don't care.

I'm lying.

I do care.

I sip my cocktail and look out over blue sky. I go back to the pad in front of me. I write. More thoughts to add to the notebook. It's really kind of therapeutic, you know? It really is.

The old dame sitting next to me has been peeking at my scribbling when she thought I wasn't looking. So what. Peek away. That's just the kind of guy I am.

"Excuse me?"

I look over at the dame. *French.* That explains the heavy kohl liner.

"I was wondewing. All zis, how you say, cheekin scwatch." She points an arthritic finger at my pad. "You air wearking vewy haird."

"I thought I'd try my hand at a novel."

"*Ah!* Zen! I was whight! You air zee whight-air!"

A writer?

I nod.

"Bwavo! Air you stwuggling? Or air you poobleeshed?"

I stare numbly, lost in the moment (and the eyeliner). Bet she hasn't washed her face since before the war. Simply keeps applying liner on top of liner, lipstick on top of lipstick.

"I'm about to be published," I rasp. "For the first time."

She elbows Harold and wakes him with the news. He leans across and extends a hand in my direction. "Congratulations, son. First story! That's swell. You're on your way."

Smiling, I shake Harold's hand. I'm on my way. Home.

"We have begun our descent into Los Angeles. Please return your seat backs and tray tables to the upright position…"

I tuck the pad into the seat pocket before me and fasten my seat belt. I look out at orange cliffs of Malibu bathed in glowing twilight. Could there, in all the world, be a more beautiful sight?

I lean against the padded headrest, close my eyes, and sigh.